SAINT IGNATIUS
AND THE COMPANY OF JESUS

SAINT IGNATIUS
AND THE
COMPANY OF JESUS

Written by August Derleth

Illustrated by John Lawn

IGNATIUS PRESS   SAN FRANCISCO

Published by Farrar, Straus & Cudahy, Inc.
A Vision Book
Reprinted with permission of Farrar, Straus and Giroux, Inc.

Cover art by Christopher J. Pelicano
Cover design by Riz Boncan Marsella

Published by Ignatius Press, San Francisco, 1999
ISBN 0–89870–722–6
Library of Congress catalogue number 98–74109
Printed in the United States of America ∞

CONTENTS

I

THE FALL OF PAMPLONA

A KNOCK ON THE DOOR woke Captain Ignatius de
Loyola on that May morning in 1521. It was not
yet dawn. Outside, the city of Pamplona lay still asleep
in the mountains of Navarre, the province that had
once been a kingdom on the northern edge of Spain,
next to France.

"What is it?" he called out.

"Captain Herrera wants to see all the senior captains at once, sir."

Ignatius grumbled. He could hear the messenger run on his way to awaken others. If only the commander, the Duke of Nájera, had not gone out to look for reinforcements to hold Pamplona, then Captain Herrera would not be in temporary command to make one jump for every little thing! Imagine, waking a man at this hour of the morning!

Nevertheless, being a soldier, Ignatius was trained in obedience. He got out of his comfortable bed, put on his colorful uniform, and sloshed cold water onto his face. By the light of a candle, he looked into the mirror. What he saw there pleased him. He was not a tall man, but he was every inch a gentleman—a true nobleman of Spain. His eyes were dark and intense. His face was finely cut, with a rounded brow and a thin mouth.

He put out the candle and left the house where he was staying.

The first hint of dawn was now coming into the rough streets of Pamplona. A few chickens were already out, together with the dogs. Ignatius walked rapidly toward the house where Captain Herrera waited.

When he arrived, three other captains had already reached the headquarters of the company that occupied Pamplona for Spain. France and Spain had been fighting a long time for control of Navarre. Sometimes the French occupied it; sometimes the Spanish were in possession. Ignatius noticed at once that everyone in the room looked glum and unhappy, including Captain Herrera, a fat man who had more taste for food than for war.

"Well, Captain Loyola—bad news", Herrera greeted Ignatius. He waved toward a thin, boyish fellow so deep in the shadows of the room that Ignatius had not seen him. "A scout from the passes."

The scout pressed forward. "A large army of the French, Captain. I saw them with my own eyes. They march on Pamplona. Where else could they be headed?"

"Then why do we wait?" asked Ignatius "Why have the fortifications of the city not been manned?"

"What good would it do?" asked Herrera. "The fortifications were not even complete when Cardinal Ximenes was replaced as the king's adviser. It was he who planned them, and those who came after him have done nothing more for Pamplona. How can we protect the city?"

"By fighting, sir", answered Ignatius promptly.

"We must surrender, Captain", said Herrera.

Ignatius was shocked. "Surrender?" he exclaimed. "While our commander is even now looking for reinforcements? Never." He turned to the other captains. More of them had come in now. "What do you say? Do I hear you speak for surrender?" Then, without giving any of them time to answer, he turned back to Captain Herrera. "To run from a common danger is the nature of cowards", he cried. "Brave men must always take the chance of dying in the ruins—that is the danger soldiers must always accept."

Most of the captains, Ignatius saw, were on his side. Only one spoke out against him. "The trouble with you, Ignatius, is that ever since you stormed and took the town of Nájera, you've seen yourself as a soldier's hero. There was a time, remember, when you wrote songs and sonnets."

"I sought no spoils at Nájera", answered Ignatius angrily. "The honor of my victory was enough for me. I did not permit my men to loot and rob. Besides, that has nothing to do with Pamplona. I say we are honor bound to fight."

Several of the captains now raised their voices in his support.

Captain Herrera motioned to them to be quiet. "Nobly spoken, Captain Loyola", he answered Ignatius "But I fear it would not be wise to fight. We're greatly outnumbered. Besides, you know the temper of the people—they're always for whatever ruler is not in power. Today Spain occupies Pamplona, so they are for France. Tomorrow it will be France, and in no time at all they'll be crying for Spain again. That is the nature of people who live on the border between two countries. I'm afraid we can't fight to success."

"But let us at least give blow for blow until we are

taken", cried Ignatius "Surely we can hold out until the duke returns with more men!"

"Do you know where the duke has gone? Does anyone?" Captain Herrera shook his head. "No one has been able to find him. The plain fact is, we can't defend the city with incomplete fortifications around it and an enemy people behind us."

"Then let us go to the citadel and fortify ourselves against attack", said Ignatius

Captain Herrera began to give in.

A chorus of voices rose from the captains. All were in favor of retreating to the citadel while there was still time.

Captain Herrera agreed. "Very well. To the citadel."

The citadel stood in the center of Pamplona. It was a round building of stone blocks. There were openings, called embrasures, in its walls, so that weapons could be used against any enemy who might attack it. It stood high enough so that the soldiers in it could see the passes of the Pyrenees Mountains to the north. It was from this direction that the enemy would come.

The Spanish hardly had time to fortify themselves in the citadel before the French appeared, making their way out of the passes. They came down directly toward Pamplona, and, without so much as a shot being fired, they began to enter the city.

By midday the French were in possession of Pamplona. The undependable people of the city were making themselves useful to the French in every way. The French learned at once that the Spanish defenders were fortified in the citadel. Heavy, lumbering cannon were drawn up in the principal streets facing the citadel, and all other preparations for an attack were made. Ignatius and his fellow captains watched grimly from behind the stone walls.

But the attack was delayed. Ignatius could see one talk after another taking place among the French officers. Finally, he saw a fluttering of white as a flag of truce was raised. A captain of the French army and two foot soldiers stepped smartly forward toward the citadel.

"We'll see what he has to say", said Captain Herrera.

"Captain D'Arcy in the service of His Majesty, Francis I, King of France", said the French officer when he was brought in. "Have I the honor of speaking to the commander of the Spanish forces?"

"You have, sir", answered Captain Herrera.

"We hope, sir, that you realize how impossible your situation is. We have come to ask your surrender", said Captain D'Arcy.

There was an immediate protest from the captains. Captain Herrera held up a hand for silence.

"We're well fortified here, as you see, Captain", he answered the Frenchman. "We're prepared to withstand your siege. Your scouts must surely have told you that our commander is on his way with reinforcements?"

Captain D'Arcy said nothing to this. He only smiled a little, as if he knew better. "Let us not look to hope, sir." He waved a hand elegantly behind him, toward the city. "We are drawn up for the attack. There are over twelve thousand of us, with thirty pieces of artillery. You cannot hold us off. We offer you safe conduct out of Navarre."

Again a chorus of angry cries rose from the Spanish captains.

Captain Herrera shrugged. "You hear my men, sir. We have no choice but to hold the citadel."

Captain D'Arcy bowed and left.

Immediately there was a great bustle of last-minute preparations in the citadel to make ready for the attack. Captain D'Arcy walked stiffly across the square to where his commander waited. From the embrasures of the citadel, the Spanish captains could watch while the French officer made his report. At first the French commander appeared to be thinking about what his captain said; then he came to life and began shouting orders. The officers around him scattered; he himself went off with some of them. There was an ominous grouping of soldiers around the cannons.

Despite all this, there was a delay of two hours before the attack began. Then the cannons began the barrage.

Ignatius turned from the embrasure where he had been watching and cried, "Men of Spain! Let us fight like soldiers. Let us die like soldiers for the honor of

Charles, our king, and the eternal glory of Spain, our country. Who dies for his honor in loyalty to his country deserves immortal glory."

The roar of the cannons drowned him out.

But there was no rushing of French troops upon the citadel. There was no one for the Spanish soldiers to fight. All they could do was to man the few pieces of heavy artillery mounted at the citadel and return a thin fire. The French did not intend to attack the fortress now; they meant to lay down a barrage of cannon fire and simply lay siege to it. So it seemed to the Spanish.

When darkness came, the cannons ceased their fire.

Captain Herrera walked up and down among his officers. "We all know we haven't enough food to stand off a long siege", he complained.

"Unless the duke returns in force", said Ignatius

"Ah, well, you, Captain Loyola—you live on hope and honor and glory, perhaps. We simple men need food. The Frenchman didn't need to say it—no one knows where the duke is. Home perhaps, even though he is the governor of Navarre."

"Sir, we could take a group of men and rush the French", said Ignatius

"Madness! They outnumber us many times." Captain Herrera shook his head.

"Then we shall fight until we drop of weariness."

"I think we will. But I've just examined the walls. The cannons have left their mark. The stones will tumble down on us before long."

In the morning the barrage began once more. The day was Whit Tuesday, the twentieth of May. The Spanish had begun it with prayer, but now they were grimly at their posts, waiting for the onrush of French soldiers. But the enemy did not come.

Toward noon, the barrage grew stronger. More and more cannon balls struck the ancient stones, and here and there cracks were beginning to appear in the walls. Just at noon, the French troops at last pushed forward. They came in at the citadel from all directions, streaming in from the side streets, shouting and waving their weapons.

The Spanish soldiers sprang into action. Ignatius was in the thick of them, firing first from this embrasure, then from that. He called out for a force of men to break from the citadel and engage the storming French soldiers, but Captain Herrera forbade it.

After the barrage had gone on for some time, a cannon ball struck Ignatius in the legs. One leg was broken completely, and the other was also damaged. Ignatius, who had been knocked down, dragged himself over to the wall, motioning away his comrades who came to help.

"Keep on fighting", he cried. "If we do not, we are lost."

Captain Herrera hurried over and knelt beside him. "I'm sorry, Captain Loyola—our surgeon has been killed."

"No matter. Let us hold fast."

But even while he spoke, Ignatius saw by the expression on Captain Herrera's fat face that the resistance was hopeless. The shouting outside had grown louder. The cannons were no longer being fired, lest the French harm their own men. Instead there was a slow, steady booming, which meant that the French had resorted to the battering ram to break down the great door of the citadel.

Ignatius tried to stop the flow of blood from his broken leg. He called to his comrades to lift him and stand him on his one leg at an opening so that he could fight as long as he was able to do so. But none listened to him. It was clear that most of them no longer cared about fighting.

Yet they held on for another hour, even a little more.

Then, abruptly, Captain Herrera ordered a cease-fire.

"Men, we must stop the fighting", he said soberly. "The door will give way at any moment."

Now not a voice was raised against his decision. Ignatius would have spoken, but he was too weak to do so.

The noise outside had stopped, too. The French knew that the citadel must surrender, and, when firing stopped from the inside, they held their own fire and waited.

Captain Herrera went back to the great door and gave the orders to throw it open and lay down arms.

The French soldiers poured into the citadel, led by that same Captain D'Arcy who had come to offer terms before the attack. He walked coolly over to Captain Herrera.

"My compliments, Captain Herrera. Have you many wounded?"

"Seventeen, by latest count. Ten men are dead, including our surgeon."

A tall, slender man came walking up behind Captain D'Arcy. Overhearing Herrera's words, he said quietly, "Captain, call our litter bearers forward."

Captain D'Arcy saluted smartly. He turned to the Spanish captain. "I present our commanding officer, Colonel André de Foix. Captain Herrera, in charge of the Spanish company."

"I thought Nájera was in command here", said the French officer.

"Gone, sir", replied Captain Herrera.

"Let me talk to your wounded, Captain."

"As you like, sir."

Colonel de Foix, following Captain Herrera, came to a stop before Ignatius. "This fellow's leg is shattered, Captain. Is he quartered in the town?"

"Yes, sir."

Colonel de Foix beckoned to Captain D'Arcy, who came at once. "See to it that this officer is carried to his quarters, and send our surgeons to set his bones", he ordered.

Then he spoke briefly to the rest of the wounded

Spanish soldiers. He told them that the French respected gallantry and would treat the wounded with every courtesy. All those Spanish officers who were not wounded would be free to make their way out of Pamplona and Navarre and return to those portions of Spain which were not disputed with France. All the wounded would be sent home as soon as their condition allowed.

Ignatius was only hazily aware of being lifted gently by French soldiers to a litter. One of his Spanish comrades-at-arms ran ahead, at Captain Herrera's order. He led the way to the quarters Ignatius had occupied before the call had come to defend Pamplona against the French.

For two weeks Ignatius lay ill. His leg healed stubbornly. True to the promise the French commander had made, surgeons attached to his company had come to attend to him. One came every few days to learn how he was getting along.

One day Colonel de Foix himself came to see him. He came in, stooping because of the low ceiling, and sat beside Ignatius' bed.

"Captain Loyola, we hear many fine things said of you", he told him. "We learn it was because of you that the citadel was defended at all."

"Sir, I only did my duty as a soldier."

"Well said, Captain. I admire gallantry and loyalty. You've been well treated at our hands?"

"I have no complaint of your courtesy, sir."

"I have good news for you. Our surgeons tell us you're well enough to travel. On a litter, perhaps—but at least you can go. I'll instruct some of my men to take you where you wish to go, if you'll tell me where that is."

Ignatius lay for a few moments in silence. He could not go, wounded as he was, to be a burden to his former commander, the Duke of Nájera. Nor could he return to the household of Juan de Cuéllar, where he had spent most of his years since he was a small boy. Since de Cuéllar's death, his estate had been broken up. Ignatius had left to become a soldier; now he could not go back. There was but one place for him to go—that was to his ancestral home, the castle of Loyola in the province of Guipúzcoa, even though his father was dead and his brother now held most of the lands.

"I will go to Azpeitia, where I was born", he said quietly.

Colonel de Foix raised his eyebrows. He did not know where Azpeitia was.

"It isn't far away", Ignatius hastened to say. "It lies just out of Navarre—not far at all to the west."

"Ah, that is Basque country."

"Yes, sir. The province of Guipúzcoa."

"I will have you taken there, Captain Loyola. You start tomorrow."

Colonel de Foix patted his shoulder in encouragement, and took his leave.

Ignatius began to look forward to Azpeitia. What would it be like to go back to the home of his childhood?

2

THE RESTLESS SPIRIT

IGNATIUS HAD NOT BEEN to Azpeitia for a long time.
He had been only a boy when he had left his home
to live with an aunt at Arévalo in Castile. His father
had sent him there. It was his father, too, who had
planned for him to go to the household of de Cuéllar,
who served King Ferdinand and Queen Isabella. Old
Beltrán Yánez de Loyola wanted Ignatius to become

familiar with the life of the court. His mother, had she lived, would surely have approved of his choice for Ignatius.

But now Ignatius' father was dead, and he was welcomed back home instead by his sister-in-law, Magdalena, and, when he returned from fighting in Castile, by his brother, Don Martin Garcia de Loyola. Both of them were alarmed at his appearance and insisted on sending for surgeons of their own choice to examine Ignatius' leg.

Ignatius protested, but his brother would not listen.

"No matter what they told you," said Don Martin, "your leg isn't healing the way it should. Those French doctors were clumsy."

And the Spanish surgeons, when they came, agreed with Don Martin.

"The leg will not bear your weight", said their leader.

"What must be done, then?" asked Ignatius

"It must be rebroken and reset, sir."

"That butchery again!" sighed Ignatius.

Just the same, he gave his consent, and when the bones were broken and set again, he bore the pain without a murmur.

In the long days that followed, Ignatius was very ill. Fever racked his body, he had little appetite, and he suffered pain day and night. During those moments when he seemed free of both pain and fever, he spoke long with Don Martin, who sat with him and asked

what he had done with his life since he had left
Azpeitia as a little boy.

Ignatius told his brother how he had left the home
of their aunt, Maria de Guevara, to go into that of
Juan de Cuéllar. He spoke to him of what he had seen
of the royal court. He told him how he had always
been drawn to the life of the sword. He had admired
the soldiers of the king, and he was soon weary of
court life, which he thought very useless. Besides, his
master, Juan de Cuéllar, had followed King Ferdinand
in death in 1517, and the time was right for a change
in Ignatius' fortunes. So, when Cardinal Ximenes,
who was the minister of state while King Charles was
in the Netherlands, called for more troops, Ignatius
had volunteered.

He had been put at the head of a company of
soldiers sent to put down a rebellion in Biscay. He had
marched to success with his company. They had attacked and taken the town of Nájera. After a short
occupation of that city, he had been sent with other
soldiers to serve at Pamplona under the governor, the
Duke of Nájera.

Of the fall of Pamplona, Don Martin already knew.

"And what will you do now, Brother?" asked Don
Martin.

"I am in duty bound to make a report to the duke,
my commander, as soon as I am able. Captain Herrera
will have told him of my wound. Then, perhaps, I
shall again become a soldier of the king."

"That will take a while, Ignatius."

"Yes, I know. This leg must first heal."

But the leg did not heal. Not only did Ignatius' fever get steadily worse, but the leg mended awkwardly. A piece of bone pushed out of the flesh just below the knee. The leg was now actually shorter than the other. If and when Ignatius got to his feet again, he would have to walk with a limp.

As June wore on, Don Martin called in other surgeons. Ignatius' condition was so serious that his life was in danger. The most notable of the surgeons, Dr. Lopez, gravely shook his head.

"If nothing changes by midnight tomorrow—or by dawn of the twenty-eighth," he said, "then I fear there is no hope."

"What of the bone pushing from his leg?" asked Don Martin.

"We shall speak of that later—if need be."

After the surgeons had gone, Don Martin leaned above Ignatius. "Brother, can you hear me?"

Without opening his eyes, Ignatius answered, "I hear you, Martin."

"Did you hear what the doctor said?"

"I heard."

"The twenty-eighth is the day before the feast of Saint Peter. If you haven't forgotten how, in your years as a soldier, pray to him that you may recover."

On that night, late in the dark hours of the twenty-seventh day of June, Ignatius woke from a fevered sleep and lay staring into the darkness. Past the stone walls around the window he saw stars winking in the heavens. His throat was parched. He was so weak that he thought neither of life nor of death, but only lay there quietly in the warm night. In his feverish sight, the darkness wavered and the stars danced. Once he thought he saw someone looking at him from the wall—a grave, almost sad-faced man, who stood in a circle of light. It was surely Saint Peter, come in answer to his prayers, for Ignatius thought he heard his voice saying, "My son, all will be well." But in a moment this was gone, the darkness was back, and Ignatius' tired lids closed once again over his eyes.

In the morning, to Don Martin's joy, Dr. Lopez announced that Ignatius had passed his crisis and that his leg would now mend. His fever was broken, and the weakness that had worn him down would soon be gone, too.

Day followed day, in endless succession.

One morning Ignatius sent word that he wished to speak with his brother. When Don Martin came, he found Ignatius wearing a troubled frown.

"Have you looked at my leg, Martin?" he asked.

"Indeed, I fear our Spanish surgeons did no better than the French", answered Don Martin regretfully.

"Martin, I am a proud man. I am a Spanish nobleman. How can I wear my hose and my boots with a bone sticking out of my flesh? How can I walk in pride with one leg shorter than the other?"

Don Martin was silent.

"Why do you not answer me, Brother?"

"There's nothing to be done, Ignatius."

"Something must be done. I wonder that life itself is worth living with such a deformity!"

"I'm sure it is, Ignatius. You grow impatient. No wonder! You've been lying here so long. I'm happy to see you with such spirit. Perhaps you would like to talk with Dr. Lopez. Let me send for him."

The gray-bearded old doctor came at once and listened to Ignatius without expression on his face. When Ignatius had finished, he answered him, choosing his words with care.

"It's true—we could perform yet another operation", he admitted. "We could open the wound and saw off the bone that pushes out. Then, to lengthen the leg, we could attach a rack to it. We could do all this—but it would be very, very painful. The pain would be far greater than any you have suffered so far. And, under the rack, you would need to lie here for many more months."

"Any suffering is more bearable than disfigurement", said Ignatius

So, for the third time, the doctors opened his leg. Ignatius bore the pain with courage, but it was so great that there were times when he fainted. Nor was the pain done with once the operation was over; it lingered long after. And the rack on his leg to stretch it back to its normal length was a thing of constant torture.

Only the thought of returning to the pleasures of the world gave him strength. He remembered many times the joys of life at the court—even though he had grown tired of that life. He recalled with pleasure his swaggering pride in his uniform as a soldier. It seemed to him that he could bear any pain if only in the end he could return to the life he had led at court and as a soldier.

But, as week followed week, there was one punishment he could not bear well. That was boredom. Now that at last his life was no longer in danger and his leg was healing, Ignatius was bored with lying in bed. He did not need to trouble himself any more about his leg, for Dr. Lopez had promised him that he would have only the slightest limp.

He spoke of his boredom to his sister-in-law when she brought his lunch one day.

"Are there no books to read?" he asked. "I die of this eternal lying here with nothing to do."

"I'll see, Ignatius", she answered.

When she came back for his empty dishes, she carried two books.

"These are all I could find."

He looked at them with eagerness, which turned quickly to displeasure. "*The Lives of the Saints* and Ludolph of Saxony's *Life of Our Savior!*" he exclaimed. "Is this fit reading for a soldier?"

"I'm sorry, Ignatius—we have no other books."

He pushed the books from him. "Take them away. Better nothing than these."

"What would you have me bring, Ignatius?" she asked.

"Why, tales of knights and their ladies", he replied. "Tales of adventure and daring. These books—why, these are women's reading, not books for men."

"I doubt if there are any others in all Azpeitia."

She left the books. She knew well that there were no others in the castle of Loyola. Since Ignatius still had many long weeks to spend in bed with a rack on his leg, he would perhaps think better of them.

Gradually, just as his sister-in-law had foreseen, Ignatius came to look upon the books more favorably. For one thing, his boredom did not end; it grew greater with every day that passed. For another, no matter what they were not, the books were at least pages of printed words to look at, instead of the unchanging walls and the view of the valley from his tower room.

So, at last, one day he took up one of the books and began to read.

As day followed day, he read steadily through the *Life of Our Saviour* and then through *The Lives of the Saints*. At first he read almost against his will. He was sure that he would not like what he read. After all, he had learned of all these matters in his childhood. He resented having to read about them again just because there were no other books to be had.

But when he had finished the books, he read them again. And this time he read with more interest. He looked upon both books with a changed vision. Time and again, he thought that the saints, too, were adventurers, even soldiers. When Saint Francis of Assisi, taken prisoner before the sultan in Egypt, preached the gospel to him, was he not a soldier of Jesus Christ? When Saint Dominic went among the Albigensian heretics to preach to them and pray for them, going barefoot and in poverty, was he, too, not carrying the banner of our Lord? When Saint Stephen defended himself before the Sanhedrin, was he not defending the glory of God? When Saint Patrick made the trials of skill with the Druids of Loigaire, was he not engaged in an adventure as daring as that of any soldier of any king? When Saint Paul stood alone before Caesar, defying his great power in favor of a greater power from above, was he not acting for his master, Jesus Christ? When Saint Elizabeth of Hungary suffered the cruelty of her brother-in-law, was she not also a soldier on Christ's battlefield?

It was strange to Ignatius that he should think this way. He had always thought first of the pleasures of a worldly life. Even now, as he read and reread the life of Christ and the lives of the saints, he thought from time to time with deep joy of the many delights he had known at the home of Juan de Cuéllar and at the court of King Ferdinand and Queen Isabella. But now he thought just as often of the saints. Just as frequently as he saw himself in his dreams as a great knight of the king embarked on some daring adventure, he saw himself as a saint, serving Jesus Christ in unknown corners of the world.

Was it possible to be a knight in both the world of the flesh and that of the spirit? He asked himself this often. While at first he thought that it could be done, gradually he came to understand that no man could serve two masters. He must be of the physical world or of the world of the spirit, if he would be a true knight. And more and more often, he told himself that if Saint Francis could walk among lepers, surely he could also do so. And if Saint Dominic could take a vow of poverty, this was not beyond Ignatius' power to do—by the grace of God.

Day after day, Ignatius was lost in dreams. He turned to the books again and again, studying them intently now, where before he had only read them. Gradually—so gradually that even he was not aware of it—he thought more often of the saints and the Master they served than he did of the gaiety of the court of the king of Spain. And he began to notice that each time he recalled the life at court—that which had once given him so much pleasure—he recalled it with less and less pleasure. At the same time, whenever he dwelt upon the lives of the saints and their adventures as soldiers of Jesus Christ, he grew just so much happier.

He began to think for the first time that perhaps he had a vocation. Did God mean to call upon him to separate himself from the world? If so, how should he do so? Perhaps he might make a pilgrimage to Jerusalem. Like Saint Dominic, he would go barefoot and in poverty. He would do many penances and would give himself up to prayer.

On another day he thought that he might become a Carthusian monk. He commanded that a servant be sent to the city of Burgos to ask about the way in which the Carthusians lived, so that he might think about their rule.

One night, as he lay in the darkness, meditating, he saw a glow upon the wall of his room. Soon, in the midst of a brightness as of day, he saw our Lady with the Child Jesus in her arms. The vision lasted but a moment—then it was gone. But for that moment Ignatius was filled with a great joy, and afterward he thought of his earlier years with the greatest disgust. He resolved that he would never again look back with pleasure upon the years he had wasted in childish merrymaking.

Donna Magdalena found him often on his knees after that night. She heard him speak much of God and the saints and less and less of his past deeds, and she spoke of this to her husband.

Don Martin was troubled. He came to have a talk with his brother.

"I feel that you are thinking of some change in your way of life, Ignatius", he said. "What is it you have in your thoughts?"

"It may be a change", agreed Ignatius

"I hope you won't betray the future honors our family has a right to expect from you. You've already given us much. You've won the favor of our king for your bravery and your abilities, as well as for your loyalty. We've hoped for much from you."

"How do you speak to me, Martin—as my brother, or as head of the house of Loyola?" asked Ignatius

"As both."

"I hope I will not disappoint you, Brother."

"I charge you never to forget that you are a Loyola."

"Whatever I do, Martin, trust me. I will never bring dishonor to our ancestors."

"Do you plan to leave us, then, Ignatius?"

"Do I have your permission to go, Brother?"

"You need not leave us. But, on the other hand, I will not stand in your way. Where do you wish to go?"

"I plan—if I may—to go for a brief while to visit our sister at Aránzazu. Then I must go to make my report to the Duke of Nájera. He's still my commanding officer. I owe him this."

"True. And when do you wish to go?"

"When I am well enough."

"The doctors say that will be in the spring."

"In the spring, then."

"We will be sorry to see you leave us, Brother."

"Thank you, Martin. Your good wife and you have been as kind to me as any man might hope for. I haven't been a good patient; yet I have many things to be grateful for—but most of all, besides your kindness, for the privilege of reading these two books, which have opened my eyes to a wider world."

3

THE SHRINE AT MONTSERRAT

I N THE SPRING of 1522, Ignatius set out for Navarrete
to make his long-delayed report to the Duke of
Nájera. He wanted to go alone, but Don Martin
would not hear of it. He sent two servants with
Ignatius. All rode on mules, because some of the
territory they would have to cross was mountainous,
and the mules were sure-footed.

The Duke of Nájera was happy to see Ignatius. He
was at the door of his rich home to meet him, for

scouts had brought him word of Ignatius' approach. He walked in with one arm around Ignatius' shoulders.

"Herrera has told me all about you, Captain Loyola", he said. "He has admitted that if it were not for you, there would have been no defense at Pamplona. And how much better to lose a battle than to be disgraced by surrendering without one!"

The soberness of Ignatius puzzled him. "But you're still ill. You're not like the Captain Loyola who came to serve under me. Have you forgotten how to laugh and joke?"

Ignatius smiled sadly. "No, sir. I am sorry Your Highness finds me so much changed."

"I do. I do, indeed. But no matter", continued the duke in a hearty voice. "I have a fine commission waiting for you. This time you'll be in charge of a large company, and there'll be no need to argue against weak leaders. You yourself will be the leader."

Ignatius thanked him with emotion. Then, choosing his words well, he added, "Forgive me, but I cannot accept the commission. I came to resign from your service after I had made my report."

"You're joking!"

"No, Your Highness."

"I swear to you that you have a bright future as a soldier. You've passed successfully every test of loyalty and courage. Perhaps it's a longer rest you need. In that case. . . ."

Ignatius shook his head. "No, Your Highness. I've turned from the life of a soldier. My face is set toward Jerusalem."

"Well, then—make your pilgrimage. Then return to us."

"I don't plan to return, Your Highness."

Nor could anything the Duke of Nájera say change Ignatius' mind.

At the end of three days, Ignatius prepared to move on. He had made his report. He had stood against all his former commander's arguments. He had been firm against the duke's rage and against his despair, too. Now he commanded the two servants of Don Martin to return to the castle of Loyola, even though they had been ordered by Don Martin to stay with Ignatius.

Then he himself set out early one morning for the shrine of Our Lady at Montserrat. He went alone, determined to pray there before starting the journey to Jerusalem. He went first to Cervera and had no company on the way, so that his mind was free to think of what his goal should be after Jerusalem. He was not yet sure; the world was still very much with him. He felt that he was still blind, but there was in him now a powerful longing to serve God as best he could—to become a soldier of Jesus Christ just as he had once been a soldier of the king.

He came soon to a mountain village, where he stopped. Because he remembered the many penances of the saints in whose steps he hoped to walk, he bought himself in this town a piece of prickly sack-cloth. This was very different from his blue mantle, yellow hose, and feathered cap. He went to a tailor's shop and had himself measured for a garment to be made of the sackcloth. It should be one that cloaked him loosely and reached to his ankles. Then he went into another shop and bought a staff such as pilgrims used. He also bought a pair of sandals made of hemp and a calabash in which he could carry water. One of the sandals he could not wear, for his bad leg was still swollen and bandaged; so he discarded that one.

Ahead of him lay the jagged peaks among which stood the shrine of Our Lady of Montserrat, together with a great Benedictine abbey. He traveled forward over dangerous mountain trails, confident that God's goodness would not let him perish.

At last, on a day late in March, Ignatius reached Our Lady of Montserrat, which stood halfway up the tall, saw-toothed rocks that towered four thousand feet into the sky.

He did not go directly to the shrine. He felt unworthy. He wanted first to make sure that he was in a state of grace. He wished to make a general confession of all his sins. He knew that there was at the Benedictine abbey at that time a monk of great sanctity. This was Father Jean Chanon. Father Chanon had once been Vicar General of Mirapoix, but a visit to the Bene-dictine abbey had induced him to give up the world and go into the monastery. There his reputation had grown. He was a saintly man whose presence added to the great fame of the abbey.

Ignatius was fully prepared for his general confession. He had begun to think about the sins of his past life long before he left the castle of Loyola. He had finally written down a long list of them, so that he would not forget even the least sin.

Father Chanon was a man in late middle age. That Ignatius should ask for him was no surprise to him. People came from many places to make their confessions, and there were monks in the abbey who could hear confessions in any language. But he was surprised to learn that Ignatius was a Spaniard, not a Frenchman.

The confession Ignatius made to Father Chanon took three days.

When at last Ignatius had been granted absolution, he confided to Father Chanon that he had decided upon a goal in life, and he asked for advice.

"I have determined to devote the rest of my life to the greater glory of God, Father", said Ignatius.

"Have you given this much thought, my son?" asked Father Chanon.

"Yes, Father. I've thought of it often. I've lain awake at night and thought only of how best I could serve God. I'm happy in no other thought. I wish to do nothing else."

"You have been worldly, my son—more so than many who confess here."

"I'm ready to do any penance, Father. The days of my worldly vanity are behind me."

"You must make up for these sins."

"I'm prepared to do so, Father."

"It is no easy life you plan, my son. Indeed, it is the most difficult of all lives. Denial is hard for the flesh, but sometimes it is even harder for the spirit. Yet it is the noblest of lives, and those who are called to it are blessed of heaven. He who assumes the staff of the Lord turns from all else. Though he remains a part of this world until his body dies, he belongs to another. Do you think, my son, that, for all the years that remain to you, you can turn away from a world you have loved so well?"

"Yes, Father. I was a soldier; I am used to obedience."

"That may make it harder for you. It is easier to obey a master you see in the flesh than one who is present only in the spirit." He smiled and added, "But we shall talk of this further, my son."

Ignatius spent many hours with Father Chanon.

At last the priest gave him his blessing and wished him godspeed, even though he was sure that Ignatius himself did not yet know his mission. But, like Ignatius, he believed that this Spanish nobleman who had sought him out had a mission that would be made known to him in time. At the moment, Ignatius thought only of the journey to the Holy Land.

All during his last day at the Benedictine abbey and

its neighboring shrine, Ignatius planned his remaining hours. As a young man, Ignatius had been influenced by a popular book he had read. This was one called *Amadis of Gaul*. It was an account of chivalry, a book about noble deeds performed by the knights who roved the countryside in search of daring adventure. It was the obligation of each knight, before he took to the road, to prepare himself by performing the vigil of the armor. This was done by praying all night before the altar of the Blessed Virgin. It was called the vigil of the armor because it was the first deed performed by a newly made knight, and the first wearing of his new armor.

Ignatius, too, wished to perform the vigil of the armor. But the fine clothes he wore were not going to be his armor in the service of God. Indeed, no such fine clothing as that worn by the knights would be his. Ignatius was troubled at the thought of wearing his gentleman's clothing before the altar, for it was not fitting that one who was determined to offer his life to serve God should be dressed in rich garments.

It was the eve of the feast of the Annunciation when Ignatius slipped out of the abbey immediately after supper. The grounds were filled with pilgrims. So also were the hills near the shrine of Our Lady of Montserrat. The pilgrims had come for the celebration of the Annunciation. Ignatius set out to walk among them, seeking one who was the most poorly clothed.

In the gathering twilight, he came upon a man whose clothing was not only poor but sadly torn. He went up to him at once and addressed him.

"Sir, I would like to speak with you privately."

The pilgrim bowed humbly at the sight of Ignatius' fine clothes. He walked with Ignatius until they were away from the other pilgrims, behind a screen of thick bushes.

"Will you change clothes with me?" asked Ignatius then.

The pilgrim drew back, alarmed. "How should this be," he asked, "that a nobleman should ask this?"

Ignatius explained his need, with great patience. He wished to give away his clothing, which was not proper to his new calling. Once the pilgrim was convinced that Ignatius was not trying to play a trick on him, he gladly agreed.

When the exchange had been made, Ignatius put on the sackcloth he had bought and made his way into the church. Now he wore the armor of his service to God.

There before the altar of the Blessed Virgin he spent the night in prayer. Sometimes he knelt. Sometimes he prostrated himself, pressing his face to the stones. He prayed for guidance. He prayed for the success of his mission. His soul was troubled because he knew that as long as he thought of himself as a knight of our Lady, he was still not free of the sin of pride. The giving away of his clothing had not yet cleansed him; it was only the symbol of his intention.

The long hours passed, and dawn came. His vigil of the armor was over.

At the early morning Mass, Ignatius received Communion.

Then he walked quietly out of the church and away from Montserrat. His goal now was Barcelona. There he hoped to find a ship that would take him on the first part of his journey to Jerusalem. He did not want to walk the main road to Barcelona, because there he might meet someone who would recognize him, and he did not want to be remembered. Besides, he did not want company on his journey, for he wished to meditate and pray as he went along. So, instead of following the road, he chose to go along a rough mountain trail. He did not know where it led, except that it was in the direction of Barcelona.

He went on foot. He left behind the mule that had carried him. It was no longer proper, he felt, that a man who had dedicated himself to serve God in poverty should own a mule.

The way was not easy, and his leg had not yet healed perfectly. He was lame and walked with a limp. After the cool dawn had passed, and the middle of the day drew nearer, Ignatius grew tired very quickly. The night of his vigil had been a great ordeal for his still weak body, and now the strain of following the steep, winding mountain path added to his weakness. He had to stop from time to time to rest. Each time, he sat down beside the path and looked out upon the beauty of the mountains set out against the blue sky. All this, he told himself humbly, as well as the eyes that looked upon it, was the handiwork of God.

But never once did he wish for his mule to ride. Never once did he ask for any relief from his weariness. He knew he would have to bear this weariness of body. He accepted it without a murmur of protest. He went on ever more slowly, and his periods of rest came more often.

By noon, when he found a shaded place beside the trail, he left the path and sat down. He knew that he must begin to think of lodging for the night, but he did not know where he was, except that he was closer to Barcelona. He would ask the first traveler he met, even though there were few travelers on this road he had chosen.

Nevertheless, as he sat there resting, he saw far down the path a party of travelers coming from Montserrat. There were four women and two young men, scarcely more than boys. He guessed that they had been to Montserrat for Mass on this feast day. If they did not come from Barcelona, they must have come from some other town near by.

As they came up, Ignatius saw that one of the ladies was somewhat older than the others. It was to her that he addressed himself as he got up.

"Pray forgive me, ladies and gentlemen. I am in

search of lodging for the night. Can you tell me where I might find it?" he asked.

The two young men rode forward on their mules as if to shove Ignatius aside, but the older woman held up her hand to stop them. Her eyes, Ignatius saw, were kind. He saw, too, that she examined his clothes with interest; the sackcloth he wore did not escape her notice.

"You speak in the accents of a gentleman. Yet you're dressed like a beggar", she said thoughtfully.

Ignatius lowered his eyes. He made no reply.

"We're going to Manresa", she went on. "That is the next town. It is but a village. Won't you accompany us?"

"Thank you. I will", he answered.

"There are accommodations to be found there", she continued. Then, seeing how he walked, she added, "But you're lame. Won't you ride one of our mules?"

He shook his head. "No, thank you. I prefer to walk."

She signaled to the others of her party and said to Ignatius, "Then we'll go slower, at your pace."

Ignatius thanked her again. He noticed how she kept her eyes fixed on him. She was filled with curiosity as to who he might be. He did not offer his name. He wished to be unknown. Above all, he did not want to meet anyone who would remind him of his life as a soldier or courtier. Nor did he want anyone to know that he was from the castle of Loyola, lest they question him.

From the conversation among the women, he learned that the lady who had spoken to him was a certain widow from Barcelona, named Iñez Pascual. She was in Manresa on business. Just as Ignatius had guessed, she and her friends had gone to Montserrat for Mass. They were now returning, and, judging from their talk, Manresa was near by.

They had not gone far when they heard someone shouting behind them. Turning, they saw one of the monks from the abbey riding after them. They all paused, including Ignatius.

"You, there", said the monk to Ignatius as soon as he caught sight of him. "Are you but lately robbed of your clothes?"

"No, Father", said Ignatius.

"We've taken a beggar dressed in fine clothes. He says a gentleman gave them to him. We have arrested him."

"Then, I beg you, free him. He has done no wrong. I gave him my clothes freely."

The monk looked at him strangely. All the women and men of the party did likewise. But none questioned him. The monk thanked him and turned to go back the way he had come. The widow Pascual only gazed at Ignatius with greater interest than before.

Ignatius returned her gaze. "I am so great a sinner

that I could not even do my brother a service without injuring him", he said sadly.

No further words passed among them.

Soon they were at Manresa. There the widow Pascual took Ignatius to a place for travelers. It was called the Hospice of Saint Lucy. She arranged for a bed to be given him and promised that she would send him food every day.

Ignatius thanked her once more. Then he turned gratefully to the bed and the rest it promised.

4

MANRESA

AFTER ONLY ONE NIGHT in the bed at the Hospice of Saint Lucy, Ignatius rejected it. The bed was too comfortable. Moreover, he felt a need to mortify his flesh still more in punishment for the wistful thoughts that came to him now and then about his former life. He wished he could forget the life he had led before turning to God. He began to sleep on the floor, using a stone or a piece of wood for a pillow.

He heard Mass every day. Sometimes he served at the Mass. He attended every other service in the church at Manresa. Every day he knelt for many hours in prayer.

Even this was not enough for him. He gave away the food the widow Pascual sent to him daily. The poor were more in need of it than he. Each day he begged in the streets so that he might learn greater humility. To remind himself always that he was mortal and must die and to punish his body for having filled him with longing for the evils of the world, he wore a shirt of hair under his loose sackcloth robe. His hair grew longer and longer, for he did not cut it, allowing it to grow as it would.

Ignatius did not intend to stay long at Manresa. He expected to be on his way within a few days for Barcelona. Then, from that port city, he would go to Italy and the Holy Land. But, in order to travel to the Holy Land, he had to have the permission of Pope Adrian VI for the journey. The new Pope was not yet in Rome; so there was no cause for Ignatius to hurry.

When at last word came that the Holy Father had reached the Vatican, Ignatius was kept from going to Italy at once by a plague—a terrible sickness—that was spreading through Barcelona. As a result, the days lengthened into months, and still Ignatius was at Manresa.

He did not complain at the delay. He was sure in his heart that it was God's will that he stay at Manresa.

Here he would have the chance to write down in the book he always carried with him more of his thoughts about prayer and about the way in which mankind could grow closer to God. Many people were kind to him. Though she had learned that he gave away the chicken and broth she sent to him, the widow Pascual continued to supply his food. The Dominican priests, who had a monastery in Manresa, gave Ignatius a cell for his own use. Whenever he did not want to go to Saint Lucy's, or whenever his bed at the hospice was needed, he had a place to go among the Dominicans. But here, too, he slept on the floor. The people of Manresa soon grew to know him, and the children, when they met him on the streets of the town, often made fun of him by calling him "Father Sack" because of the cloth he wore.

Ignatius did not mind the jeers of the children. He did not mind the disapproval of some of the older people, either. He wanted only to be left to worship God in his own way, and he was never really satisfied with his way. He did not think he worshiped God with the devotion he deserved. He felt himself tempted on all sides. He prayed constantly for guidance. He read the story of the Passion over and over, and it seemed to him that this alone gave him the greatest peace. Yet, despite the seven hours daily that he prayed on his knees, and the additional prayers he said at midnight when he woke for that purpose, he knew little peace.

Perhaps, even at Manresa, he was still too close to the world. He began to walk out of town to be alone in the countryside. One day, near the Cardoner River, which flowed by Manresa, he came upon a cave almost hidden by thorny bushes. It was almost twenty feet deep and six feet wide. Its mouth was almost eight feet high, but the ceiling came sloping down sharply inside. The bushes hid it from the sight of anyone who might be passing. Ignatius decided that if ever he needed a place where he could be more alone than in his cell at the Dominican monastery, he would return to the cave.

Soon his doubts drove him out of the cell at the monastery. He seemed to be constantly in despair. He began to believe that the confession he had made at Montserrat was not a good one. But one of the Dominican priests, to whom he confided his doubts, told him gently to stop worrying.

"Don't accuse yourself of things you have not done", he told Ignatius. "Accuse yourself only of those deeds, thoughts, and words that you know are sinful."

Ignatius was not comforted. "Perhaps I sin in the danger of growing satisfied with my mortifications", he said.

"There's always that danger, my son", admitted the priest. "But I see no sign of it in you."

"Father, if ever you see me in such danger, come to me. Say to me, 'Remember, you sinner, how many sins you have committed in the sight of God.'"

The priest promised to do so. "Now tell me, my son," he went on, "how long you have fasted."

"One time for a week. Another time for ten days."

"Why do you fast?"

"So that I may have God's help in driving away my temptations."

"They tell me you neither eat nor drink for many days at a time. We have long known you take no meat—only bread and a weak tea of herbs mixed with earth and ashes."

"That is true, Father."

"Now, my son, this is not the way to the Lord. If you injure your health, how can you perform whatever mission God may have intended for you? Unless you stop this needless and dangerous fasting, I must refuse to grant you absolution in confession. Will you promise?"

After an agonized minute of hesitation, Ignatius answered, "Yes, Father. I promise."

"Go, then, with the grace of God."

At first, in the cave near Manresa, Ignatius found a certain amount of peace. But soon all the doubts and trials he had known for so long returned to trouble him. It seemed to him that Satan himself was tormenting him. He knew that when he began to wonder whether he could bear many years of such penance, it was the inspiration of the devil, tempting him. "Better to suffer for decades than for eternity!" he cried aloud, each time this doubt of his faith came upon him.

Alone in the cave, Ignatius chose to go over his entire life again. The happy, carefree days of his childhood came back to him. But there were things, too, that he did not want to think about. There were wrongs he had done as a child and as a youth.

Then there were other events Ignatius forced himself to think of—tavern brawls, for instance. He was covered with deep shame at the memory of them, and of one in particular, when he had been with his brother and both had fought victoriously. He could still hear, ringing in his ears, the voice of the judge before whom they had been taken. "You are a young man of good family; yet you brawl like a common soldier. You ought to be ashamed of yourself, and your brother as well."

Much as he would rather not think of these events of his earlier years, Ignatius did not try to avoid doing so. There were other, greater sins. The years he had spent giving himself up to the vanities of the world were now years of shame to him. How proud he had been of his post with Juan de Cuéllar! With what pride he had walked in his fine clothes—just as, later, after de Cuéllar had died, he had worn the uniform of a Spanish soldier! He thought with shame of the sins into which his pride had led him. He had lived as others at the court had lived. Later, he had brawled with every soldier. He had thought only of winning military glory. He had wanted to be known as a great soldier and a sturdy fighter.

He had not thought of God, even in his leisure time. Then he was always writing poems, though, truth to tell, often his poems were of spiritual things. But many of them had been addressed to ladies of the court. Could he perform enough penance to erase the sins of his youth and early manhood? Ignatius now wondered.

Sometimes, in his cave, Ignatius was so disturbed in mind that he came even to doubt the value of prayer. He endured great agony of spirit. Often, when the agony was greatest, he cried aloud to God for help. "Help me, O Lord!" he prayed. "For I find no help in man or in any other creature. If there is a place where relief is to be found, no trial is too great, no obstacle too hard for me to overcome to find it. Lord, show me the way. I am your servant. I will follow where you lead."

His eyes grew hollow, and his cheeks fell in from lack of sleep. He continued to pray day and night, until it came to him that by this very devotion he was doing injury to himself and thus to the mission for which God intended him. After this, he slept longer, though his nights were filled with dreams and visions.

In his long hours alone in the cave near Manresa, Ignatius began to think of preparing certain Exercises for those, who, like him, wished to be led closer to God. These Exercises were to be ways of examining conscience, of meditating, of contemplating, even of praying. Through them, one could be brought near to

God and to an understanding of his divine will. They could be made alone. Ignatius thought it would be better, though, to be guided by someone who knew the Exercises and had studied about man and God. Then the student could be advised from week to week through all the Exercises.

At first Ignatius thought of putting down in a book of blank pages a set of simple rules. He would call them Spiritual Exercises. But the more he thought about it the more he wanted to add to the Exercises. He realized after a while that, as he learned to know more of God and man, he would add to what he now wrote, and they would grow beyond a set of simple rules.

Ignatius wanted to set down directions for making a retreat. It was his goal to help all those who wished to come closer to God. He wanted to help them attune their minds and hearts to Christ's will. If people could only know the teachings of Christ and learn to believe in them, then more and more would want to walk in the path of Christ. Ignatius believed that self-denial was the key; so first, men must deny themselves. He wrote first of repentance.

"I shall ask my soul for an accounting, from the time my eyes open to the day until this moment", he wrote one day. "I shall trace one hour after another. I shall examine one part of the day after another. I shall ask after my thoughts, I shall ask after my words, I shall demand of my deeds that they reveal wherein I have sinned. All this, before I ask pardon of God our Lord for my sins and those flaws in me which make my sins possible."

He determined that the first Exercise should be made at midnight. He himself had risen many times at that hour to pray and meditate on God and his goodness. The second Exercise should be made at the hour of awaking in the morning. A third should take place just before or just after Mass, and a fourth at the hour of Vespers. The last should be made within the hour before the day's last meal. Everyone who wished to make a retreat, thought Ignatius, should make these Exercises daily during the four weeks of the retreat, unless his health did not permit it.

Ignatius divided the Spiritual Exercises into four weeks, of which the first should be given over to repentance. The others should be devoted to the contemplation of Christ, his life, and its meaning. Above all, each man should think often of Christ's sufferings, and every man should accept the standard of Christ. He should think of how Christ chose poverty instead of riches, how he accepted contempt instead of honor, how he practiced humility, not pride.

Because Ignatius' own pride had troubled him so often, he set down his definitions of humility. He believed there were three degrees of humility. "The first lies in this, that I be humbly obedient to the law of God in all things, and not violate any commandment, whether of God or his Vicar, that binds me, under pain of mortal sin", he wrote in his book. "The second lies in this, that I am indifferent to riches, honor, and health, and that I would not bring upon myself the pain of venial sin. And the third, which is the most perfect humility, lies in this, that I desire poverty and contempt and the lowliness of fools and to be treated as Christ was treated before me."

Slowly his Spiritual Exercises grew. They were not complete. Ignatius thought that they would never be complete, for he changed so many lines he had put down. But one thing he did not change was this: "The more that the soul is alone and apart from others, the more fit it becomes to draw near to its Creator and to be united with him; and the more intimately it is united with him, the more likely is it to receive the holy grace of its Creator."

Ignatius divided his time between the cave and the Dominican monastery in Manresa. He was so deep in his meditations that he was seldom aware of what went on around him. Thus he was deeply surprised to learn from one of the Dominicans that some of the people of Manresa complained of his begging and his talk of coming closer to God. But he comforted himself by believing that God was again testing his humility and patience.

This was only the least of his trials.

Many people of Manresa, however, had been moved by Ignatius' piety. His example alone brought him followers. Ignatius did not seek them. He continued to think of himself as the least worthy of men. In the months he had been at Manresa, which added up to almost a year, Ignatius had become known as the most pious man in the town. Yet he himself thought only of how great a sinner he had been and of how many faults he still had. Some women were beginning to follow his example in attending Mass and receiving the sacraments daily. One day one of them spoke to him on the street, saying, "I pray that our Lord Jesus may appear to you some day." Ignatius was shocked and replied, "How could Christ appear to one so unworthy as I am?"

But as more and more of the ladies of Manresa began to attract attention by receiving the sacraments often, others mocked Ignatius. Evil people, Ignatius knew, were always made uneasy by the sight of goodness. Even those families who had befriended Ignatius, including that of the widow Pascual, were insulted and attacked. Sadly, Ignatius made preparations to leave Manresa.

One day, before he left for Barcelona, he went out of Manresa to sit down beside a wayside crucifix near the Cardoner River. He sat quietly, enjoying the sunlight and praying, as he usually did. He was unaware of any who passed, being deep in his devotions.

Suddenly a light more brilliant than that of the sun fell all about him. He looked up, startled. A great peace descended upon him. There, at the source of the light that almost blinded him in its intensity, was the radiant figure of God! Ignatius fell to his knees, but he could not take his eyes from the vision before him.

Then it seemed to him that God spoke to him and said, "Ignatius, you will go forth and gather together a company of men to bring all men closer to me, to save souls in all places of the earth, and to insure the salvation of all men." And God told him many more things, showing him how to form his company of followers, so that Ignatius was filled with great new understanding of God and the things of God.

Then the vision faded and was gone.

Ignatius ran to the cross and threw himself at its foot in renewed prayer. Afterward he hastened back into Manresa, where, day after day in those last days in the town, he saw other visions.

Then for a week he lay gravely ill. He was in a trance that no one could break, and, from the speech he uttered during his trance, it was clear to those who waited upon him that he talked with God.

When at last he came out of his trance, he said only, "O Jesus, Jesus!" Of what he had seen while he lay there he would say nothing.

But when he left Manresa, he was a different man from that limping beggar who had come walking into the town from Montserrat. At Manresa, Ignatius had found his mission.

5

TOWARD THE HOLY LAND

WHEN IGNATIUS REACHED Barcelona, he no longer wore the sackcloth of Manresa. He had learned that very poor clothes drew just as much unwelcome attention as very rich clothes. He had also learned, just as the Dominicans at Manresa had told him, that he must not mortify his body so much.

The purpose of his fasting, his prayers, and his going without sleep had been to put from himself all desire except the love of God. But too many mortifications damaged his health. This, in turn, weakened his determination to love God because he was not able to do so to the best of his ability. So now Ignatius wore a cloak and shoes, as well as a sombrero. This made him look like the scholars who traveled through Spain.

Though the plague had ended in Barcelona, Ignatius discovered, to his disappointment, that he could not set sail for Italy as quickly as he had hoped. There was no room left on the ships. Ignatius went every day to the harbor in search of passage. The rest of his time he spent in church, visiting the sick, or calling on monks and hermits in the city and outside the walls.

One day, as he was coming from Mass, a well-dressed woman spoke to him. Ignatius had noticed her in church, with her servant. As he came out, she was waiting for him and came directly toward him.

"Your pardon, sir", she said. "Will you do me the charity of sharing our dinner?"

"Thank you, I will come", answered Ignatius.

She introduced herself. Her name was Isabel Roser. She was the wife of a nobleman. Like many such women, she spent much of her time doing good deeds. She had noticed Ignatius the previous day at Mass, when she had seen, she thought, a kind of halo light about him. She had spoken of this to her husband, and he had told her to find Ignatius and ask him to dinner. Her husband was blind, so he had to stay at home most of the time. He took pleasure in entertaining his friends, travelers, and all those whom his wife invited to their home.

All during dinner, Ignatius talked of God and the love of God. The blind Roser listened with great interest, but he said little. When Ignatius mentioned his Spiritual Exercises, both the Rosers said they wished to make them. Ignatius promised to guide them through the Exercises if time permitted.

"Surely there is always time for a retreat", cried Señora Roser.

"I am on my way to the Holy Land", replied Ignatius. "I am even now waiting to set sail on a brigantine lying in the harbor. We leave for Italy in a few days."

"Don't go", said Roser. "We need you more than they do in Italy."

"No, I must go", answered Ignatius.

"Well, then, at least, don't go on the brigantine. Those small ships are dangerous. Our relative, the bishop of Barcelona, is leaving for Italy soon in a stronger ship. Let us try to persuade the ship's captain to give you free passage."

Ignatius hesitated. He had been promised passage on the brigantine only a day ago, after waiting for some time. Should he now wait for a better ship? The poorer his accommodation, the better suited to his spirit, he felt. Yet he could not deny his hosts.

"Thank you. I will wait and see."

It was three days before he again saw the Rosers. "The captain has agreed to take you free to Italy, but you must buy your own food", said Isabel Roser, as soon as Ignatius came into the house. "But we'll take care of that—we'll send enough food along with you."

Ignatius shook his head. "I cannot accept it. I've already accepted far too much from you."

"And your brigantine", continued Señora Roser. "It was surely God's will that you didn't sail on it. It went down only a few hours out of Barcelona. All hands were lost."

Ignatius knew of this. He had already prayed long for the souls of those who had drowned.

"The ship leaves in three days", said Roser. "How will you find food if you don't accept our gift?"

"My trust is in God, sir", answered Ignatius. They could not induce him to accept food for the voyage. He went begging through the streets of Barcelona. He took whatever was offered him, particularly hard bread, which would last throughout the voyage. Whatever coins he received, he left on a stone bench at the seashore. Whoever found them could keep them. He needed only a little food for the voyage, and he wished to go penniless in God's name.

On the fifth day out of Barcelona, the ship came to Gaeta, in Naples. There Ignatius disembarked. Three other pilgrims—a mother, her daughter, and a young man—were, like him, bound for Rome. The four of them went together, on foot, along the Appian Way. At the first place where Ignatius stopped for alms, he was repulsed with horror. "Get away from me!" he was told by those whom he approached. People drew away from him, pulling back their cloaks. He had not realized that his penances had made his face so thin that he looked very much like a person who had the plague.

It was the same everywhere.

At last he spoke to the woman among the little group. "Madame, if it please you, I will walk apart from you. All who meet us fear that I have the plague, and this may bring hardship on you, too."

But the woman shook her head. "If you had the plague, you would have died long ago", she said. "It is no matter. We'll soon be in Rome. There you will go your way, and we will go ours."

Pope Adrian was now in residence at the Vatican. When they reached Rome, Ignatius went at once to Saint Peter's and begged for an audience with the Holy Father. He had to wait but a day before being allowed to see the Pope, in the company of other pilgrims.

Adrian VI was a man in his sixty-fifth year. He did not seem well, and he was plainly aging. Ignatius would like to have spoken to him, but he did not dare to hope for a private audience. He knew that many things troubled the Pope, especially the continual attack on

Christian countries by the Moslems. Only a few
months before, at the end of 1522, the Moslems had
fallen upon Rhodes, a Christian island ruled by the
Knights of Saint John, and were now in possession of it.
The Pope was still calling in vain for Christians to unite
and repel the Moslems. The marks of the Pope's an-
guish were clearly to be seen on his careworn face.

He spoke briefly to the pilgrims as he granted them
licenses to visit the Holy Land. Then he gave them the
Papal blessing and returned once more to his problems.

Ignatius did not hasten from Rome.

He visited many churches. He begged in the streets.
Whenever he had the chance, he spoke to all who
would listen to him of God and the glory of loving
God. He made many friends, for there were always
those men and women who tried to be closer to God
and yet could not separate themselves from the ways
of the world. These people always befriended men
like Ignatius, who could cast off the world. Perhaps
this was because they knew that they could not do as
much, and so they admired those who could.

Some of them told Ignatius that he must take
money along to the Holy Land. They said he could
not hope to reach Jerusalem without gold in his
pockets, so they persuaded him to accept seven gold
crowns. He was to sail for the Holy Land from Venice.
But he had no sooner started for Venice than he began
to scold himself for his lack of faith. How could he

have had so little trust in God's protection as to take gold along to the Holy Land? After lying in troubled sleep all one night, he could hardly wait to give away the seven gold crowns to the first beggars he met.

It was almost twice as far from Rome to Venice as from Naples to Rome. It was hard for Ignatius to travel, though he soon fell in with companions who were bound for the same city. The many penances that Ignatius had endured at Manresa still affected him. He was weak and often ill, though he bore both weakness and illness without complaint.

Ignatius and his friends were not welcome anywhere. The plague still raged throughout Italy. The people were afraid of travelers because those who moved from place to place might carry and spread infection. No one wanted to receive them into his house. Often they were not even permitted to pass through villages on their way; they had to travel through the fields on the edge of the villages.

They were forced to sleep under the stars. But this did not trouble Ignatius at all. Even as a boy, he had loved the stars. He had spent many hours watching the heavens. Now he felt more than ever at home with the stars. Were they not all God's handiwork, just as this earth was, on which he lay? When it rained, the travelers found places in old sheds or under hedges.

They reached the Venetian country at Chioggia. There they were told that if they wished to enter the city of Venice, they must have certificates that showed that they were free of infection. They must go to Padua to be examined by the doctors there. But this Ignatius could not do. He was now so feeble that he could not make this extra journey and still hope to reach Venice. So he bade his companions farewell. They went on to Padua, while he stopped to rest.

That night in his sleep Christ appeared to him and spoke. "Be of good faith, Ignatius", he said. "Nothing shall stand in your way."

When at last Ignatius reached the city of Venice, he learned to his great joy that the certificates of freedom from infection were no longer needed in order to enter Venice.

But there were other troubles he had to conquer. Because he had given away all his gold, he had nothing left for a night's lodging. Nor could he beg easily, for he could speak no Italian. In Rome, many people had understood Spanish, but in Venice, he found few people who knew his language.

He fared so badly in trying to ask alms and looking for a place to sleep that when night came he still did not have a bed to lie upon. He went to a passageway, lay down in the open on the stones, and, saying his prayers, fell asleep.

He had not been sleeping long when he was awakened by a touch on his shoulder. He sat up, blinking his eyes against the light of a pair of lanterns held above him. He heard someone speak in Italian, saying the name of Senator Trevisani.

A man in early middle age came forward to look at Ignatius, while the other men, who seemed to be his servants, stood aside. This man spoke to Ignatius. Again the language was Italian.

Ignatius answered in Spanish, saying that he was sorry he could not understand.

But Senator Trevisani understood and replied in Ignatius' own language. He introduced himself and asked, "What is your name?"

Ignatius told him.

"Ignatius de Loyola", repeated the senator. "I must remember that. Now you must come to spend the night at my home and stay there while you are in Venice."

"Our Lord has seen fit to let me lay my head here", said Ignatius.

"Your pardon, sir", answered the senator with spirit. "Our Lord has made other plans for you. Only this night, as I lay asleep in my bed, a voice spoke to me out of the darkness, saying, 'How is it that you sleep in comfort in your bed, when my poor servant lies on the bare stone near by?' I arose immediately, called my servants, had the lanterns lit, and looked for you. You are the man. You look like his servant. Let me serve God in so little a way as to offer you a bed. Besides, you look ill and half-starved."

Senator Trevisani was a man accustomed to giving orders. But no order would have moved Ignatius. Had it not been for the senator's strange experience, he would have remained where he lay. He rose humbly, marveling at the way of God, and walked with the senator and his servants toward the house, which was not far away.

All the way the senator talked. Had Ignatius eaten? What was his mission in Venice? He asked so many questions that Ignatius was glad when he could sink quietly into the fine bed to which the senator's servants showed him.

But in the morning, all happened as before. His conscience bothered him. How was it that he, who had made a vow of poverty, should live in such luxury? He could not keep his vow and, at the same time, live as Senator Trevisani wanted him to live. After a simple breakfast at a generously laden table, Ignatius thanked the senator but refused his offer of free lodging and food until his ship sailed for the Holy Land.

Senator Trevisani was amazed. "But you're not well now. You may become even more ill, sir. Surely he who woke me in the night and sent me in search of you does not want you to beg in the streets and endanger your health. He sent me because you might well have died in the night."

Nothing would move Ignatius. His conscience would not let him accept the senator's offer. He left and took up his former life. He spent his time begging once more. He went visiting the sick. He knelt for hours in churches in every part of Venice.

Slowly he learned a little of the Italian language. Begging became somewhat easier for him. But no way to the Holy Land was open to him. Nevertheless, as the days lengthened into weeks, which became months, Ignatius did not despair. He was supremely confident that all in good time God would make known his wishes for him. So he went his way, often with so little food that he was in fever for days at a time.

Then one day he met a merchant from Guipúzcoa, his own home province. He had known him a little from his earlier years, and the merchant, Simon Contez, recognized him on the street.

"Something told me to look well at you", he cried. "I wouldn't otherwise have known Ignatius de Loyola. You look in want. Come along to my house and have dinner with me."

Ignatius was, in truth, weak for lack of food. He went along, not for the food, but because he knew that Contez might know of ships sailing for the Holy Land. Over a simple meal, he explained his need to Contez.

"Well, there's the admiral's ship", said Contez. "They're taking the lieutenant governor to Cyprus in a few days. But, of course, you couldn't go on that."

But when, later, Contez wanted to give Ignatius food and clothes, Ignatius refused them, asking only one thing. "Get for me an interview with the Doge." The Doge was the chief official of Venice.

"Ah, I see—you're going to try for the admiral's ship, after all. You've lost none of your ambition, Ignatius, even though it now seems to follow a new direction. This can be done."

Within a day, Ignatius stood before the Doge of Venice, Andrea Gritti.

"Your Highness, I am a poor pilgrim, under the vow of poverty, on my way to the Holy Land", he said. "I come as a beggar to ask you to help me get free passage on the admiral's ship. For two months I have begged in the streets of Venice, and God has not deserted me. I beg now this last thing of Venice."

The Doge, an elderly man, fingered his beard thoughtfully. His eyes were troubled. Before he answered, he turned to one of the men in the council room. "He does not look well. Examine him, doctor", he said.

The doctor stepped forward and examined Ignatius.

"He has a grave fever, which accounts for his wasted appearance, Your Highness", said the doctor. "If he desires to be buried at sea, he can surely make the journey."

"My hope is in God", answered Ignatius calmly. "I have been ill before. I will be well again."

The Doge looked at him long and soberly. Then he waved his hand, saying, "I will order it done. Prepare for the journey. Three days from now—on the fourteenth of July."

6

JERUSALEM

ON THE LAST DAY of August of that year, 1523,
Ignatius landed at Jaffa. His joy at setting foot
upon the land of the New Testament was too great for
him to express, except in tears. Jaffa was the port for
Jerusalem and was one of the ancient cities in the
world. This was the place where Saint Peter had lived
for a while; it was here that Saint Peter had raised
Tabitha to life again, and where he had had his most
remarkable vision.

Though Jaffa still bore the marks of its attack by the Moslems almost two hundred years before, and though it was still in the hands of the Moslems, which grieved all Christendom, Ignatius saw nothing of this. It was enough for him that he had at last reached the Holy Land, as he had vowed to do.

Ignatius and the others set out without delay for Jerusalem, riding donkeys. Ignatius rode, for the most part, without paying attention to the other pilgrims. He did not hear their chatter; his thoughts were elsewhere.

As he rode along, he became ever more sure that it was God's will that he begin his mission now. True, in his visions at Manresa, he had not learned the place where his mission was to begin. But it could hardly be at a more fitting place than Jerusalem. The more he thought of this, the more certain he became that it was meant to be. He did not know to whom to apply for permission to establish his company of Jesus in Jerusalem, but this he would find out.

He was so concerned with his plans and so happy to be in the Holy Land that he went along without even noticing the great heat, nor did he hear the complaints of the others. He was eager only to reach Jerusalem.

Early in the morning of September 4, they came within sight of the city. It stood in the morning sun high on its plateau, south of the Judean hills. Because the sunlight was falling upon the city, Jerusalem seemed to glow with the brightness of some inner light. One of the pilgrims, who had been to Jerusalem before, pointed out the Mount of Olives, which was separated from the city by the valley of the Kidron.

Ignatius trembled with the anticipation of setting foot inside the city.

But Jerusalem was still some distance from them, and the donkeys moved no faster here than they did out of Jaffa.

As they neared the city, a party of riders came toward them. One of them stopped and called out, "Are there Spanish among you?"

A large number of the pilgrims were Spanish. They immediately raised their voices.

The horseman introduced himself as Diego Manes and offered them advice. Others of his party spoke to other pilgrims in their native languages.

"Examine your consciences", he told them. "And do not enter this holy city chattering like magpies."

The pilgrims became silent at once, looking a little ashamed.

Ignatius had hardly been aware of the voices about him. He heard only that voice within him which was concerned with his hopes and prayers. Now he moved closer to Manes.

"Pray tell me, sir—who governs in the city?" he asked.

"Why, the Turks, of course", said Manes, surprised that a pilgrim should not know.

"That much I know", answered Ignatius patiently. "I mean, who is in charge of the sacred places?"

"The provincial of the Franciscan Order is the Custodian of the Holy Land, pilgrim", answered Manes. "It is he whom the Turks hold responsible for all that happens within the sacred regions."

Ignatius thanked him and rejoined the other pilgrims.

The party went on. The city was now just ahead.

They had begun to climb toward it when a group of Franciscans came walking past. One of them looked severely toward the pilgrims and said quietly, "Our Lord walked before He rode."

The pilgrims at once slid off their donkeys and finished the rest of the journey on foot.

Ignatius was overjoyed, now that he was at last in the city where Jesus himself had walked. He could hardly hold back his tears. He wanted to leap for joy. He had never been so happy.

He went from place to place among those sites mentioned in the New Testament, filled with unspeakable bliss. In the Garden of Gethsemane, he prostrated himself upon the earth and kissed the ground where Jesus had suffered. Tears blinded him, but they were tears of joy.

Day after day he haunted the holy places of the city. He grew more and more determined that he would never again leave Jerusalem. He would spend the rest of his days here, founding the company of which God had spoken to him in the vision at Manresa.

Once he had made up his mind, he set about to achieve this goal.

He inquired, but he was told that he must have the permission of the Franciscan provincial just to stay in Jerusalem. The Turk officials would not even speak to him. He belonged to the "Latin nation". He was not one of their subjects. They tolerated him and people like him in Jerusalem only because the Sultan Omar had promised the Latin Patriarch that Christian pilgrims would be permitted to visit there.

Ignatius found himself at last at the Franciscan monastery.

But when he asked to see the Father Provincial, he was told that the provincial was on a visit to Bethlehem. He was expected to return before many more days had passed. Ignatius was asked to explain what he wished to ask of the Father Provincial.

Ignatius spoke of his hope to found a company of Jesus. "I wish to show to the world that the battle is not between him who is Christian and him who is not, but for mastery of the soul within every man", he said. He spoke of his Spiritual Exercises, of his way of winning souls closer to God. And he told the listening Franciscans of his dream of being allowed to spend the rest of his life in Jerusalem.

The Franciscan fathers said nothing, though the one who took the place of the provincial said, "If you like, you may stay here with us until the Father Provincial returns."

"I have but a few days left. Then the other pilgrims—my companions—must go back", said Ignatius. "Will he come before then?"

"We do not know."

Ignatius smiled. "But, of course, he will. God will send him back in time to hear me."

"Will you stay among us?"

"Thank you, no. I wish to be in the holy places." Untroubled, and sure of the provincial's early return, Ignatius continued to visit and pray at the holy places of Jerusalem. Often, on his knees, he forgot himself in his dream of establishing that company of his mission, as God had commanded him. He walked alone and apart, but he was never alone in spirit. He slept as little as he dared, and he ate seldom, so that none of his time in the holy city would be lost.

The days passed. Finally, on the day on which the pilgrims were to leave, a Franciscan came in search of Ignatius.

"Father Provincial is back. He wishes to speak with you", he said.

Ignatius returned to the monastery with him,

The Father Provincial of the Franciscans, an aging, tired-looking man, waited for him. His eyes were half-closed, and there was a patient little smile on his almost bloodless lips.

"I am told you wish to establish a new order or

some such company of men", he said to Ignatius. "I
have been given your words, exactly as you spoke
them here. Tell me, how do you propose to accom-
plish this mission of yours?"

"I mean to establish a company of men who are as
devoted to Jesus as I am, and as obedient to the
authority of Rome", answered Ignatius. "We shall go
forth and bring others to God."

"How?"

"We shall preach in the streets and in the houses. We
shall give advice. We shall guide people through the
Spiritual Exercises."

The Father Provincial shook his head slowly. "I
understand you, Loyola. I sympathize with you. This
wicked world is sadly in need of you and your kind.
But I cannot give you the permission you ask. There
are various reasons for this. Chief among them is
this—the Turks would not tolerate any preaching
such as you plan. We Catholics live here only by the
permission of the Turks. If you were to stay, you too
would have to be silent. Could you do so? I doubt it.
The power of the Turks is absolute, and we are helpless against it. If a pilgrim visits any place where he
may not go, or if he walks where it is forbidden
pilgrims to walk—why, the Turks may seize him.
They may kill him at once or sell him into slavery.
True, we have ransomed some of these unhappy
people—but we have so little money, we cannot ran-
som them all."

Ignatius tightened his lips in rebellion. He said nothing.

"I hope you understand", said the Father Provincial.

"Forgive me, Father. I have decided to stay. I wish to stand by my decision", answered Ignatius.

"Even if, to do so, you must offend God?" asked the Father Provincial gently. "You would surely offend God if you stayed against my will. I alone have this authority from Rome. I have the power also to excommunicate those who do not obey me. If you like, I will show you the order from the Holy Father."

Ignatius, saddened, bowed his head in submission. "No, Father. I will go", he said. "It is not God's will that I remain, or he would have made it possible. I was guilty of presuming to know his will."

He went out at once and joined the other pilgrims.

Even so, he was not content. A spark of rebellion burned in him still. He wished to go to the Mount of Olives once, alone, without other pilgrims, and without guards and guides. One could see there what were believed to be the last footmarks of Jesus before He rose into heaven. Ignatius wished to visit these footprints without other company. He knew very well that every pilgrim was required by the law to have a Turk for escort.

Yet he went out alone. He approached the guards and asked to go to the Mount of Olives by himself. They would not listen to him. But at last he showed them a penknife. Seeing that they were interested in it, he bribed them with it, and they pretended not to see him slipping past them to the holy place.

There he knelt to pray, kissing the earth again and again. His heart was heavy because he had to leave the Holy Land. He knelt there as long as he dared; it was almost time for the pilgrims to leave.

While he was hurrying away, someone sprang upon him, shouting angrily. Ignatius did not resist. He saw that it was not a Turk but an Armenian, whom he recognized as a servant of the Franciscans. This Armenian jostled him all the way back to the monastery, where he explained in an angry voice what Ignatius had done.

"Foolish man", said the Father Provincial. "Vain man. Is this how you serve God—to place in danger all the Christians in the Holy City? Let us hope fervently that no one else saw you, and that the guards do not speak of what you did. Your love for God is rash, Loyola. Your zeal is great, but never again let it endanger the lives of others. Go, and God be with you."

Ignatius accepted the Father Provincial's sharp words because he knew that he deserved them. He was filled with sorrow.

He rejoined the other pilgrims and reluctantly turned his back on Jerusalem. Back to Jaffa they went, and from Jaffa to Cyprus. At Cyprus Ignatius tried to get free passage on a great ship preparing to sail for Venice, but all requests were in vain. He turned then to a little ship that stood near by; its captain gladly gave him passage. And all through the long voyage, Ignatius studied and read the Bible.

And as he read and thought about what he read, it seemed to him that, even though he had a great love for God, he lacked in understanding. And if this were so, then how could he lead others to God? This troubled him throughout the voyage.

It was January of 1524 when Ignatius returned to Venice. Snow and cold chilled him to the bone. He had long ago given away his cloak. All he wore were coarse breeches, a rough doublet—badly torn—and a threadbare coat. He had nothing at all on his legs. He set about to beg again.

Within a day he met his old Spanish acquaintance, Simon Contez, once more. The Spanish merchant came upon him, as before, on the street.

"What!" he cried. "You're still here? Weren't you in the Holy Land?"

"I'm back", said Ignatius.

"And poorer than ever, as anyone can see. You'll freeze in such thin clothing. Come along. I'll give you something to wear or money to buy it with."

Ignatius went with him. Whatever he might receive could be given to those who were poorer than he, and especially to those who had not the courage to beg for their needs.

"And what are you to do now?" asked Contez. "You surely don't intend to spend the rest of your life begging!"

"By no means."

"Then what?"

How should he answer him? thought Ignatius. But he need tell him nothing except the truth. "I expect to serve God", he answered.

"It's a poor way to serve God—by begging."

"It's only now that I beg for material things", Ignatius answered him. "I beg, too, for things of the spirit. Soon I hope to beg only for souls."

Contez was generous with him. He gave him not only a piece of cloth with which to have a warmer cloak made, but also a handful of gold pieces.

That night, as Ignatius lay trying to sleep, with the cloth folded over him to keep out the cold, he thought of what Contez had said to him, He remembered, too, his doubts on the return journey from Cyprus. It was true that he could not advance toward his goal simply by begging and praying. He must do more. He must not expect God to work a miracle for him.

It grew clear to him, as the hours of darkness passed, that love of God was not enough. No, he must join love with reason, for there were men who could not be moved by reason alone but who would be moved by reason if it were joined with love. And how else could he learn to reason except by study?

He determined to enroll in school like any beginning pupil. He intended to obtain the education he had neglected in his carefree childhood and youth.

But to do so, he would have to return to Spain. He could not hope to begin his schooling without knowing the language of the school, and he did not know the language of Italy.

In February of that year he left Venice. His goal was once again the city of Barcelona.

7

A SCHOOL IN BARCELONA

As soon as he reached Barcelona, Ignatius went to
see Isabel Roser.

"I have failed", he told her. "I meant to begin my
company of Jesus in Jerusalem, but I was not permitted to do so."

"The world is wide", she answered. "It was not the
will of God. But you don't look well. How have you
fared?"

"I make no complaint. I made my way across Italy with hardly any trouble. I was taken by both Spaniards and French on the way", said Ignatius. "They are fighting about something again. The French treated me well, but the Spanish thought I was a spy. After an interview with me, though, an officer ordered me set free again, saying, 'Can't you idiots tell a fool from a spy?'" He smiled at the memory of it, and his eyes twinkled.

Señora Roser, too, laughed. Then, sobering, she asked what his plans were.

He told her he meant to go to school.

"I have just the tutor for you", she said. "Geronimo Ardévol!"

But Ignatius shook his head. There was a Cistercian he had known at Manresa, a wise old man. Perhaps he would be his tutor.

Señora Roser knew how useless it was to argue with Ignatius. She let him go on to Manresa without further talk.

In a few days he was back. The Cistercian had died. Even so, Ignatius decided, he was not yet ready for the tutor, Ardévol. He had now decided to enter school like any ordinary pupil.

"But you're thirty-three!" she cried. "That's nonsense."

"Not nonsense," answered Ignatius, "but discipline."

When he left her, he went to the home of the

widow Pascual. She, in turn, listened to his plan. She did not approve of it any more than Isabel Roser did. Just the same, she called her brother, Father Antonio Pujol, and persuaded him to give books to Ignatius so that he might go to school.

Ignatius entered himself as a pupil in a school in Barcelona.

There he sat, day after day, among boys who made jokes about him and often teased him. They laughed at his slowness to learn. It was true that their way of learning was right for boys, but it was hard for Ignatius, who was no longer a boy. Ignatius tolerated them with patience, for he knew that this was how schoolboys were—quick and ready to tease, even though they made it harder for him.

Nevertheless, Ignatius persisted. By going to school, he showed his deep desire to learn, so that he could support his arguments for the love of God with reason. But this was also an exercise in humility and in self-discipline. He who loves God, Ignatius knew, must be prepared to accept any course, no matter how lowly, that leads to heaven.

He studied hard, but he learned slowly. Soon enough he was ready for the tutor, Ardévol. He needed him. He found it too hard to keep up with the boys in his class. This was not because he was naturally slower to learn. It was because Ignatius insisted on adding his studies to everything else he wished to do. He still visited the sick in the hospitals of Barcelona;

he spent many hours in prayer on his knees. He slept no more than was necessary for him. Whenever possible, he preached to the people in the streets of the city. There was simply not enough time to do all the things he wanted to do.

One day when he was with Ardévol in the church of Santa Maria de la Mar, he spoke of his work.

"I have so many faults, my good Ardévol, that it is a miracle I should be able to learn at all", Ignatius said.

"True. But what man has not?" answered the tutor calmly.

"But mine are so much more serious in the eyes of God."

"You do yourself an injustice. You are earnest, and you have the will to learn. You're too busy at other things to devote as much time to your studies as they need. That is it."

"I knew I needed punishment", replied Ignatius at once. "I beg you, when you find me inattentive in the future—beat me just as you beat your other pupils."

"It is one thing to beat a boy, and another to beat a man", said Ardévol.

"Then I will beat myself", said Ignatius.

"I believe you would, too", admitted Ardévol, looking at him closely.

"I would. I've done it before this. I must learn. I must let nothing stop me. For myself I care nothing. I want only to bring many people to that love of God which surpasses all else in this world."

After that Ignatius studied with greater attention. Gradually he found the work easier. He began to add to his knowledge and was thankful that this favor had been granted him.

Meanwhile, Ignatius lived in the house of the widow Pascual. Her son, Juan, had become as close a friend to Ignatius as her brother, Father Pujol. Ignatius attracted much attention, without trying to do so. True, the women who tried to follow his example sang his praises. But his example was open to all. The piety of Ignatius seemed to know no bounds. Prayer and fasting appeared to be his chosen way of life. Charity was his vocation, and he often begged and carried home what he was given only so that he could give it later to the poor of Barcelona.

But there were people in the city, as always throughout the world, who had no love for change in their way of life. They fought reform, and they resented Ignatius and his success. Just as Ignatius attracted followers, so he also drew enemies just because his goodness made them feel uncomfortably guilty about their bad way of life.

He grew used to being insulted and jeered at in the streets. He was even resigned to the mockery of servants in the Pascual household. When Iñez Pascual finally learned of this situation, she sent for Ignatius.

"Tell me, is it true that my servants have spoken ill of you?" she asked.

"It is true."

"Then I will punish them and dismiss them."

"I beg you not to", said Ignatius. "After all, they only called me a great sinner, and I am that. Speak to them, if you like, but don't punish them otherwise, for that would only hurt me."

She agreed, but unwillingly.

Among the daily burdens assumed by Ignatius was that of praying before the altar of the church of the Convent of the Angels. This church stood not far outside the gate of San Daniel. Ignatius went there to kneel in prayer for the nuns, because he had learned that they were not as holy as they should have been. Soon he was preaching to them, as well. The nuns listened; impressed by his words, they began to abide once more by the strict rules of their vocation.

Sometimes Ignatius was accompanied to the convent by Father Pujol. One day, as they were approaching the San Daniel gate on their way back to the city, they were attacked by two Moors who appeared suddenly from behind some bushes. The Moors began to beat them, raining blows upon them.

Father Pujol fell, gravely wounded. Ignatius would have gone to his aid, but he was already fighting for his life. Within moments, a great blow stunned him. He, too, fell, and all went black before his eyes.

When he came back to consciousness, Ignatius lay in his bed. Iñez Pascual, dressed in black, stood beside his bed.

"God be thanked!" she cried. "Your life, at least, has

been spared." Tears filled her eyes. "My poor brother is dead. What happened? A miller found you lying beside the road at the gate of San Daniel and brought you in."

As best he could, Ignatius told what had happened. He had no doubt that some of his enemies had hired the Moors to kill him. But he would not mention their names. After all, he could not be sure, and by praying for them he might bring them to salvation. Neither Iñez Pascual nor the police could persuade him to name those he suspected.

He grieved for Father Pujol, but he himself was still too sick to be moved. And each day he grew weaker.

The weeks of his illness stretched into a month. He received the last Sacraments. His friends came to weep at his bedside. But Ignatius was sure that it was not God's will that he die before he had completed his mission. He held stubbornly to life.

At last he began to improve a little. Yet it was almost two months before he was able to get to his feet once more and walk about. And even then he was weak from staying in bed.

The attack on Ignatius had made him think that he must be about his mission. He had been looking for young men who could help him in his task. There had been three who had come to him—Calisto, Arteaga, and Diego de Cazares. Ignatius thought that they might serve with him. A fourth who came he would not permit to join. He told him that he would later accept a son of his. When Juan Pascual asked to join him, Ignatius rejected him too, telling him it was not God's will that he join them.

Nor was Ignatius at all sure of the perseverance of those first three young men who had applied to him. He continued to feel that Barcelona, like Jerusalem, was not the city in which God intended him to establish his Company and fulfill his mission.

One day, two years after he had begun his studies in Barcelona, Ignatius was sent for by Ardévol.

"You've studied enough here, Ignatius", said the tutor. "You can do no more. You're ready for higher study—perhaps at some university."

Ignatius was deeply grateful. "But where to go?" he cried.

"First there are your examinations, do not forget", said Ardévol. "Once they're over, you can think of going on. However, don't worry about them; you'll surely pass. Have you thought of any university?"

"The one at Alcalá. It's the only school I know that has funds to help poor scholars," answered Ignatius.

"Thanks be to Cardinal Ximenes of blessed memory! It is a good school. Not as old, of course, as Salamanca—but then, it is to Salamanca as the child is to the parent."

Ignatius did worry about his examinations, even though he need not have been concerned. He felt that he was unworthy. The two years in school had been slow to pass. To study among boys half his age and less had been a great trial, but he was sure that the Lord intended he should suffer. Now he stood before a group of schoolmasters, all of whom were well versed in Christianity and the study of Catholic doctrine. He answered all their questions and showed himself a good student. The masters declared him ready for any college or university that he would like to attend.

Ignatius spent a few last days in charity work. He went, too, to thank those who had helped him, especially Isabel Roser and Iñez Pascual. Nor did he forget his patient tutor. Then he spoke to those young men who wished to follow him. He told them to get ready to go to Alcalá as soon as they could do so. He himself had waited long enough.

It was in August of 1526 that Ignatius reached Alcalá, eager to begin his studies. But when he applied at the university, he learned that courses did not begin until the middle of October.

Ignatius was told that he could go to one of the inns established for students, if he wished. But this he did not want to do. He wanted more freedom to be with his companions. He wanted to come and go as he pleased, so that he could continue his charities. Moreover, he had instructed his companions in the giving of the Spiritual Exercises, and he himself hoped to bring as many people to God as he could both before and after the university term began. So they would all need their freedom. Ignatius chose instead to stay for a while at the Hospital of Antecana.

Then he went to live in the home of the warden of that hospital.

Ignatius and his companions had agreed to dress alike in Alcalá and wherever they went afterward. They had decided on a simple gray tunic, which made them look like pilgrims, for many pilgrims wore this kind of clothing. This coarse gray cloth soon caught the attention of the people of Alcalá, and many began to call Ignatius and his companions "the men in sacks".

Their dress was not the only way in which Ignatius and his followers drew unwelcome attention. Most of the time they went along carrying on their backs great bundles of all kinds of things—clothes, rags, plates, candlesticks—which they distributed in many places. Often they were followed by jeering young men. Once a local constable followed Ignatius to a house in a poor section of the city. After Ignatius had gone, the constable went to ask who he was, but none knew.

Ignatius, to his great joy, found opportunities to give the Spiritual Exercises. Sometimes he spoke to little groups in the streets. Sometimes he gathered about him people who were in the hospital. He was almost in rapture as he gave his listeners the Spiritual Exercises and instructed them in Catholic doctrine.

One day he was approached by a splendidly dressed young Frenchman who had been a patient in the hospital. He introduced himself as Jean Juanico—a page to the governor of Navarre. He was curious to

know about Ignatius' way of life. Though he was at
first filled with doubt, he made the Spiritual Exercises
and listened with increasing respect to all Ignatius had
to say.

When Ignatius had finished, he asked humbly,
"May I join your Company?"

"I will think about it", answered Ignatius.

In a few days, Ignatius told him that he would be
accepted on trial as one of the companions. Juanico,
filled with joy, hastened to give up his position so that
he could wear the gray tunic.

On another afternoon, while Ignatius was preaching to a group of patients in the hospital, he saw a
priest watching him. Soon the priest came closer to
listen. When Ignatius had finished, the priest stayed to
talk with him. Ignatius felt that the priest was un-
friendly.

"By whose authority do you preach?" asked the
priest.

"By God's", answered Ignatius without hesitation.

"By what right do you interpret Catholic doctrine?" pressed the priest. "I heard you point out the
detailed differences between mortal and venial sins. Is
that not a matter for those who have special permission to do it?"

"Have I spoken in error?" asked Ignatius then.

"I heard none", admitted the priest. "But all Spain
is filled with heretics."

"I am not a heretic, Father."

"Worse yet, there are those who would change little things here and there in doctrine and offer it as a new way to heaven."

"My only authority is God's," answered Ignatius, "and in all things I bow to the wisdom of the Holy Father in Rome."

The priest said no more. He turned on his heel and went his way without even bidding Ignatius goodbye.

Ignatius was troubled, not only by this questioning, but by many other things. He knew that ever since he and his companions had begun to walk among the people of Alcalá, there had been a growing unfriendliness to them. Some of those who opposed them were people who objected to reform; others suspected the intentions of Ignatius and his companions and thought they were not honest. Ignatius expected some move to be made against him and his followers, but he did not know what form it would take.

Late one night he was roused from bed by his host.

"There's someone to see you, Ignatius", said the warden, his eyes turned aside.

Ignatius did not ask who it was. It was plain that his host was afraid of the visitor.

At the door stood two officers, one of whom addressed Ignatius when he saw him.

"You are Ignatius de Loyola, late of Barcelona?"

"I am."

"Come with us. You are under the arrest of the Inquisition."

Ignatius turned to his host. "Do not be fearful. I will return."

Then he went quietly with the officers of the Inquisition.

8

IGNATIUS BEFORE THE INQUISITION

T HE INQUISITION was a court of inquiry autho-
rized by the Pope. It was under the rule of the
bishops in all countries except in Spain. There the
Inquisition had been established by King Ferdinand in
1480, with the approval of Pope Sixtus IV. Most of
the Inquisitors were priests, but some laymen skilled
in questioning prisoners were also employed. The
Inquisition was under diocesan direction, and various

Inquisitions were held in all the great cities of Spain. It was the duty of the Inquisition to discover heretics and to punish them.

Ignatius could not imagine what the Inquisition could want of him. He knew that all kinds of heresies existed in Spain. Some of the converted Moors had a very different idea of Catholicism from what was permitted. There were all manner of religious beliefs being taught; many of them were contradictions of Catholic doctrine. The Inquisition was duty bound to investigate everything that seemed at all unusual when it touched upon religious belief.

There was no Inquisition at Alcalá. Since that city was in the archdiocese of Toledo, it was necessary to send an examiner from there. Until he came, Ignatius had to wait in prison. His friends could see him. He could do what he liked with his time. But he had little freedom, for he could not leave Alcalá until the Inquisition had finished with him.

Some days passed before Ignatius could be brought before the Inquisitor. In the meantime, Ignatius continued his way of life as before, except that now he was in prison. He prayed even more while in prison. He was not troubled by his arrest. He was sure that God was trying him again. He was sending another mortification to test the quality of Ignatius' love for him.

At last the Inquisitor, Don Alonso de Mexia, came from Toledo.

Ignatius was brought from the prison to stand before him. Don Alonso was a man in middle age, with
small, cold eyes. He did not appear to be very much
interested; he even seemed a little bored. But he
looked at Ignatius as if he disapproved of him.

The questioning began without delay.

"Do you call yourself a priest, Loyola?" asked Don
Alonso.

"I call myself only God's humblest servant", answered Ignatius. "I have never, on my oath, led anyone
to believe I was a priest."

"Do you preach?"

"I talk to the people, and they talk with me."

"Is it not a fact that you talk of religious matters?"

"I talk of the love of God, of the need for the
spread of the love of God."

"By whose authority?"

"Is it necessary for a Christian to have authority
from any man to speak of Christ?" asked Ignatius.

Don Alonso wrinkled his nose. "You call yourself a
Christian. Do you recognize the Pope?"

"As God's Vicar on earth."

"Do you yield to the authority of the Holy Father?"

"In all things."

Questions of this kind were thrown at Ignatius for
hours. He answered them promptly and well.

On the second day of questioning, Don Alonso was
easier in his manner with Ignatius. He seemed more
friendly.

During the third day, Don Alonso turned to his advisers and snapped, "I can find nothing wrong with this man. Why am I always disturbed and sent for without cause?"

He closed the hearings and announced that he was returning to Toledo.

Yet Ignatius was not set free. He was taken back to his cell. There he sat for five days more. Then he was brought before a new Inquisitor. This time it was Juan de Figueroa, who represented the archbishop of Toledo. He was a fox-faced man whose eyes seemed to burn with an inner fire.

Like Don Alonso, Figueroa started out determined to find theological error in Ignatius' way of life. He began by covering all the ground Don Alonso had already covered. This wearied Ignatius, but it did not discourage him.

Finally the Inquisitor came to something new. Leaning forward intently, he asked Ignatius whether he knew two ladies of Alcalá named Mana del Vado and Luisa Velasquez.

"Yes, my lord", answered Ignatius.

"These ladies came to you for advice?"

"Many people come for advice, my lord."

"Did you advise these ladies to devote their lives to traveling from one hospital to another, visiting the sick?"

"No, my lord. I advised against their doing so."

"Yet they have done so. Their guardian has complained of this, and that is why you were held until I came."

"My lord," answered Ignatius, "I am not responsible for their conduct. Let their guardian speak out, for it is his responsibility. I told them not to go."

"Let that be for the moment. Do you know Don Francis Lancofia?"

"Yes, my lord."

"Is it true that you invaded his home and spoke to him of the error of his ways?"

"Has he brought a complaint against me?"

"No."

"Then what passed between us does not concern your lordship."

Figueroa gave him a sad smile, because he knew that what Ignatius said was true. He had no right to ask how Ignatius had turned Don Francis from the sinful way of life he had led.

"Do you preach on the kinds of sin?" asked Figueroa then.

"My lord, I do not preach at all as you understand preaching. If I say 'I preach', I mean that I have a conversation with someone. I talk to people in the course of having dinner with them or as you and I talk now. I do not make sermons. I talk of God and the love of God; I speak against sin and the evil life."

"I have heard of these things you have said."

"My lord, have you found error in them?"

"No, I have not."

"Then let us speak no more of them."

"Remember, Loyola, you have taken an oath to tell the truth."

"My lord, it is an offense against God to lie. I cannot do so."

"Tell us, then, do you claim authority other than that which comes from the Pope?"

"I claim only the authority of God, and the Pope is his Vicar."

The questioning went on for days.

At the end of one day, Figueroa told Ignatius that he found it disturbing that Ignatius and his followers should all go about dressed alike. "It is just as if you belong to an order, but you do not."

"No, my lord."

"Would it not be better, then, at least to wear several colors?"

That night Ignatius dyed his gray robe black. Soon Figueroa inquired about Ignatius' studies. "Do you take certain courses, Loyola?"

"I go to such classes as I like", answered Ignatius. "Since all the lectures are free, I go from one to another. I study the physics of Aristotle. I study the theology of Peter Lombard. I study many things."

Finally, after days had passed, Figueroa sent for Ignatius so that he could hear the verdict.

"We find you guiltless in your life and in your teaching, Loyola", said the Inquisitor. "You are free to leave the prison. But we forbid you and your followers to hold any further conferences, at least until you have all finished your studies in theology. And, within ten days, you are all to lay aside the habits you wear and put on the clothing of students."

Ignatius thanked Figueroa. "I appreciate your lordship's finding us free of guilt", he said. "But as for our clothing—we've already dyed our gowns, and that ought to have settled that point. What you now order, we are unable to do, because we haven't the money with which to do it."

"Nevertheless, it must be done."

"My lord," Ignatius went on, "we are of no order. We've taken no vows of obedience. Your lordship has no right to order us to wear different clothing."

"I have spoken", said Figueroa, and Ignatius understood that this was the order of the Inquisition of Toledo.

Free once more, Ignatius was determined to find some way around Figueroa's command. It was useless to argue with the Inquisitor. He had made up his mind. However unjust his decision was, he would not change it. Ignatius learned that the archbishop of Toledo was then at Valladolid. He set out at once on the long journey to that city to see him.

Archbishop Alonso Fonseca received him with kind respect. He treated him not as one who was asking a favor but as a guest. He was not yet an old man, but his hair was beginning to gray at the temples. He had shrewd gray eyes and a wide, thin-lipped mouth.

"We hear much of you, Loyola," he said, "and there are events that disturb us. Like that matter of the merchant, Lopez de Mendoza, of Alcalá."

"I do not know him, your excellency", said Ignatius.

"One of your friends asked him for money and clothing for you after your release", explained the archbishop. "He swore you were a mischief maker. 'May I be consumed by fire if that fellow doesn't deserve to be burned at the stake!' he is reported to have said. That very night, as he was preparing fireworks for a celebration, Mendoza accidentally set fire to some powder and died—of fire. We do not like the sound of these things."

Ignatius said nothing. He was dumb with misery that anyone should have perished on his account.

"But you have come for another reason", the archbishop went on.

"Your excellency has heard the verdict of your vicar in my case; so you know he has ordered us to change our clothing. This we cannot do, for we have no money, and we have taken a vow of poverty. We beg for a repeal of the sentence."

"I will gladly arrange to have the sentence repealed, Loyola", answered the archbishop. "But there are certain ways to do this. First, you must make a formal appeal."

"That I do not wish to do." Ignatius patiently gave his reasons. The appeal would cost money. Then, too, he and his followers had been given a certain length of time in which to comply with the order. The time would be up even before the formal appeal could be heard.

"Well, then, what will you do—since you leave me helpless to do as you ask?"

"It is plain I cannot go back to Alcalá", said Ignatius sadly. "But I am far from finished with my studies. Perhaps I could go to Salamanca."

"Splendid, splendid!" exclaimed the archbishop. "I have many friends there. I will give you letters to some of them. And I think you will find that there is money to be had if you are a poor student—poor, that is, in material things, but rich in things of the mind."

Ignatius did not return to Alcalá. He went directly from Valladolid to the ancient city of Salamanca, to attend the first university that had been built in all Spain. He was sorry to leave Alcalá, where he had made many friends. But the accident to Mendoza had upset him. He feared that many people in Alcalá would associate him with it, however unjustly.

At Salamanca, Ignatius was outside the power of the Inquisition of Toledo. Nevertheless, the sentence passed on him and his followers was binding wherever he went in Spain. Sadly, he begged for clothing, and, when he found something he could wear, he gave away his gown. Calisto, Cazares, and Arteaga, who had followed him to Salamanca, did likewise. Since the clothing they received by begging was very poor and ill-fitting, they attracted attention by the odd way in which they were dressed.

Among the friends Ignatius made at Salamanca were the monks at the monastery of Saint Stephen. One of them was his confessor. Ignatius had not been in the city a month before his confessor asked him to come to the monastery for dinner. He told Ignatius frankly that the subprior of the monastery was curious about the way he and his followers lived, and he wished to know more about them,

Ignatius did not go alone. He took Calisto with him. The two of them enjoyed a pleasant meal. Afterward, however, the subprior and two of the monks led the way to the chapel of the monastery. There they began to ask questions of Ignatius.

At first the subprior's questions were innocent enough. He wanted to know why Ignatius and his followers were so strangely dressed. Ignatius told him. He asked about Ignatius' studies. Ignatius told him of his work at Barcelona and Alcalá and of his hopes for Salamanca.

"I am a sadly uneducated man", he admitted.

"How can you preach, then?" asked the subprior.

Once again Ignatius explained patiently that neither he nor his followers preached, as the monks understood it. They only talked in the manner of conversation among people about God and the love of God.

"How do you speak of these things?" persisted the subprior.

"Why, we talk of virtues in such ways as to help people to love and practice them. We speak of vices so as to help people to hate and avoid them."

"If, as you say, you are not educated, you have not been taught these things in our schools. You must then have been instructed by the Holy Spirit. How is this?"

Ignatius thought a long time before he answered. It seemed to him that the subprior was asking questions he had no right to ask. He began to feel that the subprior's questions were very much like those of the Inquisition. So he said, "Father, it would be better if we spoke no more of these things."

The subprior became so angry that he ordered Ignatius and Calisto locked up until he could notify the Inquisition in Salamanca. Ignatius and Calisto submitted to the authority of the subprior and did not try to escape.

For three days they remained at the monastery. The monks had various feelings about the prisoners. Some were against them; some were for them, knowing that the subprior had no right to keep them there.

At the end of three days, Ignatius and Calisto were taken to the prison of the Inquisition in Salamanca. The Grand Vicar, Father Frías, had reached the city; he had come because the subprior had sent for him. Ignatius and Calisto were not alone in their cell; Cazares and Arteaga were also brought in and put with them. All four were chained to a pillar in the middle of the cell. There they stayed all that night, sleepless, because the rats in the prison constantly bothered them.

The next day the questioning began.

One after another, they were taken before the Grand Vicar. Calisto, Arteaga, and Cazares were questioned first. Their answers were innocent and simple, and it was plain to Father Frías that Ignatius was indeed their leader.

The questioning of Ignatius was the same as it had been at Alcalá. He was weary of it, but he did not show impatience. One point after another was taken up and satisfied. Father Frías worried a little because Ignatius told some of his listeners the difference between mortal and venial sins.

"My lord," said Ignatius thoughtfully, "surely it is not whether or not I am qualified to speak of these things that is to be decided, but the truth of them. I do not question your right to judge. I ask only that you should decide whether what I have said is true or untrue. If it is untrue, then condemn what I have said, but do not condemn me."

The Grand Vicar was so disturbed by Ignatius' challenge that he did not meet it. He asked Ignatius instead to deliver a talk on the first commandment. Ignatius at once did so.

He moved the Inquisitors so much that they could not go on with the questioning. They spoke Ignatius with great respect and encouraged him.

Just the same, the Grand Vicar did not order the

release of Ignatius and his followers. They were taken back to the prison. There they waited for the sentence of the Inquisition.

The days passed. The prisoners were not alone much, except at night. Many people came to see them. Whenever Ignatius was asked how he could bear such sufferings when he did not deserve them, he answered cheerfully, "It would be a sign that there is little love for God in my heart, if I thought it so bad to be in chains for his sake. Salamanca could not hold all the chains I would wear for love of God."

After three weeks, Ignatius and his followers were released. The Grand Vicar found them not guilty of the charges. Nevertheless, he said that they should no longer try to tell people the difference between mortal and venial sins. Ignatius was discouraged; how could he talk of good and evil without doing so?

That night he talked for a long time with his followers. Could they hope for justice in Salamanca any more than in Alcalá? It was true that many of the people believed in them and in their mission, but the authorities of the Inquisition did not wish laymen to give spiritual direction. They must go elsewhere.

But where? Would there be any difference anywhere in Spain? The Inquisition was all-powerful. Wherever he would go in Spain, Ignatius knew that the Inquisition could find him. He did not fear the inquiry of the Inquisitors, but he would never be able to complete his education if he were constantly interfered with. Worse, if he had to obey the Inquisition, he would not be able to carry on his mission; he would not even be able to continue his talks.

There was still a great center of education that was not too far away—just over the Pyrenees, the mountains that separated Spain and France. That was Paris, and now it loomed above Alcalá and Salamanca like a magnet to draw Ignatius.

9

PARIS

IGNATIUS REACHED Paris on the second of February, 1528. This time he did not come penniless. He had learned through bitter experience that the search for enough food to keep the body in health did harm to the spirit, especially if one wished to study. Before he left Spain for Paris, his friends in Barcelona had given him a purse of money—more than twenty gold crowns. This money would enable him to find a room near the university.

Ignatius arrived in Paris amid rain and sleet. The city was dreary with dampness. Nevertheless, for Ignatius the day was bright and full of promise. He made his way to the group of schools and colleges that make up the University of Paris. There he made arrangements to attend classes. Students came from all over to attend the university, one of the greatest in the world.

But he was uncomfortable carrying with him so much money. He was not used to such wealth, and he did not like to carry it. He had taken a room at a little inn near the Seine. Among the students there was one named Ferdinand Mazores, a Spaniard like himself. Mazores seemed to be such a likable fellow that Ignatius was drawn to him. Moreover, he was poor, too. One day it occurred to Ignatius that he could trust Ferdinand Mazores to keep his gold crowns for him. Mazores accepted the gold and promised to guard it well.

Happily free of this responsibility, Ignatius went about preparing for his studies. He began to think of some way to bring his Spanish followers to Paris. Perhaps he could use some of the gold from Barcelona to do this. The more he thought of it, the more likely it seemed. So, when the rent at the inn came due, he approached Mazores for his money.

Mazores' face fell when Ignatius spoke to him. Because he had such a long, thin face, darkened with a growth of whiskers, he looked terribly sad.

"Alas! my friend," he told Ignatius, "now we are both poor. I had no idea you'd need the money so soon. I've spent it—and what's worse, I can't pay it back."

"It wasn't yours to spend", said Ignatius gently. There was nothing to be gained by scolding Mazores. Perhaps Ignatius should not have been so trusting. What was done was done; his money was gone. This settled the problem of his followers in Spain—Jean Juanico, Calisto, Arteaga, and Cazares. Without delay, Ignatius sat down and wrote them. He told them to finish their studies at Alcalá or Salamanca and not to come to Paris; things were too hard in Paris. He was sorry to have to do this, because he already knew them well enough to see that they were weak. They might fall away from the practices he had instilled in them unless he were near. But if this should happen, then it would be better to lose them now.

For himself, the loss of his money was more serious. Now once more Ignatius had to go begging in order to live. He left the inn at once. He could not pay the rent and could stay there no longer. He had to find other lodgings, and he found them at last in a poor-house across Paris from the college where he studied. There he had to obey the rules of the house, which forbade anyone to leave the place before dawn or after dark. Since one of Ignatius' classes started before dawn, and another ended after dark, this meant that he had to miss two of his classes. It meant, too, that he would have less time to go begging and to give the Spiritual Exercises.

But he would not abandon the Exercises, no matter what happened. He asked himself often, with great patience, how many more tests the Lord would put upon him. Sometimes it seemed to him that God was trying him so often in order to fit him especially for his mission. Yet the way in which the Spiritual Exercises were received repaid him for much of his misery.

One of the first in Paris to make the Exercises was Juan de Castro, a student from Toledo. After he had finished them, he sold all his possessions, gave away the money received from this sale, and took the vow of poverty, telling Ignatius he was going to follow his way of life. So did two other young students from the College of Saint Barbara. Ignatius had not in any way tried to get them to follow him, for it was forbidden in the Exercises to do so. Yet, because he was older than the students, he was widely praised because he had brought them closer to God. On the other hand, he was criticized, too.

At the college one day, Ignatius learned that Ferdinand Mazores, who had robbed him of his money, was lying ill and penniless at Rouen. Ignatius, who had just come back from a begging visit to Flanders, immediately set out to walk to Rouen.

It took him three days to reach there.

He found Mazores just as he had been described— sick, lying in bed, with no one to turn to. Mazores was amazed and yet happy that Ignatius had come to see him.

"Can you ever forgive me for having wronged you?" he cried.

"I forgave you long ago", answered Ignatius. "Let us see what can be done for you now."

He went out and begged for Mazores. Then he found passage for him on a ship to Spain. Finally, he wrote letters to Calisto and Arteaga, instructing them to help Mazores when he reached Spain.

He had no sooner finished this when a letter came for him from Paris by messenger. Ignatius opened it in wonder. As he read it, he was almost in despair. Once again someone had complained of him to the Inquisition. This time Pedro Ortiz—the tutor of two of the students who had sold their possessions to imitate him—and Rector Govea of the College of Saint Barbara had lodged a complaint.

He lost no time in hurrying back to Paris.

He dared to think that God loved him to put so many trials before him. Yet he was confident. As soon as he reached Paris, he went to the Inquisitor, Matteo Ori.

"I learn that charges have been laid against me, my lord", he said. "I wish them to be looked into without delay."

The Inquisitor was a friendly and just man. He was surprised that someone should want to face an investigation. He promised to conduct an early inquiry.

"What is the nature of the charges?" asked Ignatius.

"It is not usual to say, as you know", answered Ori.

"But I will tell you. They say that you have influenced de Castro, Peralta, and Amadores, students here, to sell their possessions and take the vow of poverty."

"I know these students, but I never advised them to do such a thing", said Ignatius. "My lord, please look into the matter, so that I may be free to take the philosophy course at the College of Saint Barbara."

This time Ignatius was not placed under arrest. And within a few days he received notice from the Inquisitor that the examination had found Ignatius not guilty of the charges made against him. The three students, however, had been persuaded to change their ways once more and give up the vow of poverty. Ignatius was free to do as he liked.

That summer, Ignatius went once again to Flanders to beg from the wealthy Dutch merchants. When he was ready to return to Paris, he had begged enough money to make it possible for him to leave the poorhouse and live at the College of Saint Barbara itself.

He came back to Paris in October of that year, 1529, to begin his course of philosophy. He could not afford a room of his own, so he found one to share with two other students. One of these was a quiet young man from Savoy, named Pierre Favre. Ignatius found him very open-hearted and friendly. The other was a fellow Spaniard, Francis Xavier, who came from Navarre, near Ignatius' home province of

Guipúzcoa. Xavier was an advanced student, and he seemed to prefer to be much by himself. He was not at first as friendly as Favre, and he did not know what to make of Ignatius, who was the oldest of the three.

They got along well together. At first the discussions of philosophy and of divine matters were between Ignatius and Favre. Xavier kept out of them. He said nothing while Favre told of his early years: how, as a shepherd in Savoy, he had longed for an education—how, as a boy, he used to preach to the people of Villaret, where he was born—how, when he was but twelve years old, he had taken a vow to serve God. Xavier expected to be a teacher of philosophy, but in the meantime he had made a name for himself in university sports. Perhaps because neither the gentle Favre nor Ignatius cared much for sports, Xavier kept himself aloof from them. Yet Ignatius was so strongly drawn to both of them that he was soon convinced they were meant to join him.

All seemed to be going well with Ignatius. He found his studies much easier. He was in happy surroundings. Yet trouble stirred for him. His reputation in the College of Saint Barbara had grown. Even if he did not have as much time to give the Spiritual Exercises as before, he found many young men who wanted to imitate him and did. On one occasion he disturbed the entire college when he went to visit a plague-stricken hospital. There he helped to care for the sick, and then he returned to the college, exposing the students and professors to the plague.

Ignatius' own tutor, Father Pêna, scolded Ignatius one day. "Do you know, my son, that you are upsetting the entire college with your way of life?" he asked. "Why don't you tend only to your own affairs and let the other students go their ways?"

"Father, I'm doing only what I have been told to do", replied Ignatius. "I go my way, but they also want to go my way."

Not once, but many times, Father Pêna argued with Ignatius. Nothing was changed. At last, impatient, Father Pêna complained of Ignatius to the rector, Govea. After his talk with the rector, Father Pêna went sadly back to Ignatius.

"My son, the rector has ordered that you be punished", he said.

"I'm used to punishment, Father", answered Ignatius.

"I am sorry, but the rector has said that in the interests of college discipline, you must be publicly birched."

Ignatius flushed with sudden anger. "Punish me if you will, Father, but do not disgrace me", he cried.

"The rector has ordered it done."

"When is it to be?"

"In the morning, before all the students."

For most of that night Ignatius prayed, not for relief

of his punishment, but that his cause might not be disgraced. He did not mind being birched, but he did not think that he had earned a public lashing.

In the morning he rose early and went straight to the office of the rector. Outside, the students were gathering for the birching. Govea, a stern-faced man with brooding eyes, was surprised to see him.

"You should be outside, Loyola—not here", he said.

"I came to speak to you first", said Ignatius quietly, "about this public whipping. Believe me, for myself I could wish for nothing more than to bear punishment for the sake of Jesus Christ. I have suffered chains and imprisonment for him. I would willingly do so again. I have never spoken a word in my defense. I would not permit anyone to speak for me. I have borne punishment gladly for our Lord's sake.

"But I ask you now, is it an act of Christian justice to disgrace a man who has committed no crime but to work for the love of Jesus Christ? Can you answer to God that you have been fair in putting this shame upon me? Will you risk turning away those I have tried to bring to God?"

The rector's face showed that now he was not sure. He was troubled. "I had not thought of it like that, Loyola", he admitted.

"I don't ask for myself. I don't ask for my honor. I ask only in the interest of the salvation of many souls", continued Ignatius.

The rector rose, nervously clasping and unclasping his hands. He walked up and down his office. From outside rose the voices of the students who had gathered for the show. A few impatient ones called out for the birching to begin.

"God has willed it that my cause—which is surely the cause of all Christian men—is so well known that such a punishment as you have ordered will surely reflect upon it", Ignatius went on.

"Say no more, Loyola", ordered the rector.

Govea stood for a long minute at the window, staring down at the crowd below. Then he suddenly turned and left the room, ordering Ignatius to remain.

Soon Ignatius heard him speaking in the courtyard. The sound of his voice was followed by a great silence. Then the shuffling of footsteps began and grew louder. The students were moving away.

The rector came back. "I've cancelled the birching, Loyola", he said curtly. "You and I must speak of your way of life some time. I confess I am greatly interested in these matters, and Pêna is also. I hope, however, that you will try your best to persuade students to go to important classes. If they follow you about, command them to attend to their studies. You can do neither more nor less. That is all."

Ignatius thanked him and left.

He resolved to obey Govea as best he could. Yet students continued to follow him, anxious to know from his own lips what he believed. They realized that people seemed to be moving farther and farther from the Christian way of life, and they were eagerly looking for some way to grace.

One day Pierre Favre told Ignatius that he wished to make the Spiritual Exercises. Ignatius was delighted, and he gladly guided him through the Exercises, taking great care; he was filled with hope. Favre was as good a student as Ignatius had known he would be. Indeed, in his great zeal, he worried Ignatius a little, for he fasted too long, and he began to kneel in the courtyard by night, away from the fire, to punish himself with the cold.

"And how many are there with you now?" asked Favre one night.

"Alas, but one. I am alone. I had three, but they were lost to me in Spain. And again three, who were taken from me", answered Ignatius.

"Then let me be the first in your Company!" cried Favre.

Ignatius was overjoyed. "I've been waiting for you", he said. "And let my first command to you be to eat more regularly and stay a little closer to the fire. There will be fire enough for us to walk through before we are finished."

10

THE MEETING AT OUR LADY OF
MONTMARTRE

WHEN FAVRE HAD BEEN WON, Ignatius turned his efforts toward persuading the second man he hoped to enroll in the Company. This was Francis Xavier, who was now lecturing in philosophy. Xavier had always been a little scornful of Ignatius. Ignatius was not an athlete, and he had to struggle more to learn things that came so easily to Xavier and to Favre.

Besides this, Xavier had made great plans for himself. Whenever he did talk of his future, he always saw himself as a great teacher with many students at his feet.

After Favre's conversion, Francis Xavier seemed to be even more critical of Ignatius. He seemed to feel that Ignatius was only an odd person like others in Paris and in the great cities of Europe. He thought little of Ignatius' achievements in studies.

One evening in 1531, when Ignatius and Xavier were alone in their room, Xavier told Ignatius in confidence that he had just written to his brothers in Spain. He wished legal proof that he was a noble.

"Is it then so important to you that the world should know you have noble blood in your veins?" asked Ignatius.

"I wish such a document, yes", answered Xavier. "It may help me in the future. But what would you know of this, Ignatius?"

"Why, it interests me to know how men think. And philosophers—or teachers of philosophy, at that. You know," he went on gently, "I, too, come from a noble line. I've never thought it important to know where a man comes from so long as I know what he himself is. Perhaps you have a future greater than you know, Francis. Perhaps this document you now seek may be of aid to you, but I doubt it. I am reminded of the words of our Lord when he said, 'What shall it profit a man if he gain the whole world and lose his own soul?' "

Xavier was upset, not because of Ignatius' manner, which was friendly, but because he could see the truth in what Ignatius had said. Without saying so in words, Ignatius had made him see that what he had just done was an act of vanity grown from his pride.

But Ignatius had seen the flush on Xavier's face. "No, I don't mean to scold you, Francis", he continued. "I know you are a proud man, and why shouldn't you be? You have such an easy way of passing all the examinations, and for me they're so difficult. If you are proud, it is but a passing fault. I, too, was once proud, even vain. With the grace of God, I've left that behind me. I ask nothing now but to serve God."

Xavier smiled. "I'm afraid I haven't always been a comfortable roommate, Ignatius", he said. "And yet you've always been at my side—to lend me money when I had none, to help me find pupils, to assist me in many other ways, out of the goodness of your heart. Why?"

"Because it is God's will", answered Ignatius.

"I'm really confused by your goodness, Ignatius. There's nothing in the philosophy of Aristotle to account for it."

"You have been looking into the wrong philosophy, Francis", replied Ignatius.

"Indeed, when I think of it, it seems to me you have always served me, like a patient friend", Xavier continued.

"I serve only God. I wait on you."

"I don't miss your meaning, my friend. I'm afraid you will wait a long time."

Ignatius only smiled.

But after that evening, Xavier was more friendly. Gone was his attitude of being superior. Gone was his aloofness. Now they were three friends together, he and Ignatius and Favre. Whenever possible, he helped Ignatius with his studies, as did Favre, who was now studying for the priesthood.

And so the months passed. The year gave way to another and another. On March 13, 1533, Ignatius was able to pass the examination that gave him one degree. Now he had to study for the more difficult examination a year later. If he passed that one, too, he would become a Master of Arts.

The attitude of Xavier changed slowly but steadily. Gradually he showed an ever deepening interest in Ignatius' mission. He spoke to him about it more and more often. Then one day, with quiet decision, Francis Xavier told Ignatius he wished to give up teaching philosophy and join the Company of Jesus.

He too made the Spiritual Exercises, and his zeal astonished Ignatius. Even though members of Xavier's family—who had finally sent him the document he had asked for—now wanted him to come back to Spain for a career there, he refused to leave Paris and Ignatius. And the document he had requested he now tossed aside as worthless. Like Favre, Francis Xavier took a vow of poverty, giving up all for love of God.

Now the Company of Jesus was a company of three. Not long after, while Ignatius walked one afternoon along the Seine, he was greeted by two young men. They called to him in Spanish and seemed delighted to see him. One was scarcely twenty, and the other did not seem to be even that old.

"Are not you Ignatius of Loyola?" the elder one asked, as they hurried up.

Ignatius said that he was.

"We've come to Paris to find you. God has guided us well. I am Diego Laynez, and this is Alfonso Salmeron", he went on. "We heard much of you in Alcalá. We were students there while you were still at the university. Once or twice we saw you there."

"And now that you've found me, what next?" asked Ignatius.

"We expect to study here at the university", Laynez answered. "And we want to know more of your Company of Jesus."

Ignatius walked along with them, questioning them and answering their questions. They were alert young men, zealous and eager to learn, and anxious to advance in the world. But already they were more than half in the world of the spirit, and Ignatius found his interest in them growing with every step. He resolved to guide them as much as possible.

He found lodging for them. He spent as much time as he could with them. Even though they were young, they had been well educated at Alcalá, and they were ardent in their studies at the University of Paris. Each, too, believed that he had a vocation to follow Ignatius, and all Ignatius' questions and challenges could not sway them.

It was not long before Ignatius accepted them, too, into the Company of Jesus.

Now that it had at last taken seed and begun to grow, the Company of Jesus continued to draw members. At first there had been but one—then the three who had failed him—then the three who had been taken from him. Now they were five.

Soon there was another. This time it was Nicholas Alfonso, whom everyone called Bobadilla. He had no family name; so he was given the name of the village in which he was born. He himself sought out Ignatius.

"I came to study theology," he said to him, "but I find there is more of it to be learned from one named Ignatius than in all the University of Paris. I have taught philosophy at Valladolid, but I'm more a wandering scholar than a professor. And now I am a student once more."

"Who sent you to me?" asked Ignatius.

"No one, unless it was God", answered Bobadilla promptly. "Do you think you are not known in Spain? I heard of you in many places before I came to Paris."

After many questions, Ignatius was satisfied. He accepted Bobadilla into the Company of Jesus. And

Bobadilla, in turn, drew into the fold the sixth Jesuit, a friend named Simon Rodriguez, who was a Portuguese nobleman.

So now they were seven.

Ignatius sought yet one more. In his visits to the hospitals, he had met a man from Palma, Majorca. His name was Jerome Nadal. From his talks with Nadal, Ignatius could see he was a man of great brilliance. They spoke often of the Company of Jesus. Ignatius continued to visit Nadal after he had been discharged from the hospital. So did Laynez and Favre, who had also taken a liking to him.

One day Ignatius took Nadal with him to an abandoned church. When they were alone, he asked him to join the Company of Jesus.

But Nadal shook his head. He held up his Bible, saying, "I stand by this book; it is enough for me. If you have something better to offer, I will follow you. Otherwise I will not."

"You will follow me," said Ignatius confidently, "even if not yet."

Nadal would not change his mind, and that night Ignatius spent many hours on his knees asking God's forgiveness. He had tried to force Nadal to a vocation for which he was not yet ready.

At Easter of that year, 1534, Ignatius passed his final examinations and became a Master of Arts.

Now it was time to think most seriously about the future of the Company of Jesus. Ignatius went to visit the members of the Company who were not with him each day, and he told them to fast and pray to prepare for the decisions they would have to make. All were to meet on a day and at a place he would set. At that meeting they would decide their future course.

The day of the meeting was the Feast of the Assumption. Before dawn on that day in 1534, they met and went to the Church of Our Lady of Montmartre, a deserted church that was the site of the martyrdom of Saint Denis. Ignatius opened the meeting with a short prayer.

Then he spoke of his plans. "I hope to go to the Holy Land and live there under vows of poverty and chastity, serving God. I hope that all of you will wish to go with me."

"We do", chorused his companions.

Ignatius went on. "But I have found, from my first visit there, that there may be difficulties in our way. We may not be able to stay in the Holy Land." He told them what had happened to him on his visit, and he added, "If this is the way things are there, what shall we do?"

There was some discussion before Favre proposed the solution. "Let us then take a vote among the seven of us. Let the majority rule. And let us resolve to abide by the vote of the majority. Either we shall stay in the Holy Land despite the hardships there or return to Rome and put ourselves in the hands of the Holy Father to do with us as he likes."

"And when shall we begin the journey to the Holy Land?" asked Bobadilla.

"There are certain matters to be taken up", answered Ignatius thoughtfully. "For one thing, some of us have not yet completed our studies. I have finished. Francis Xavier has ended his work at Paris. Favre has been ordained for three months and is permitted to stay with us. But others of us have not finished their studies. It would not be right to go before they are finished. All should be finished a little less than three years from now. Could we not then meet somewhere early in fifteen thirty-seven?"

"At Rome?" suggested Rodriguez.

"Not yet", answered Ignatius with a smile. "Besides, that is out of our way,"

"In Venice, then", said Laynez.

"In Venice, in January", said Ignatius. On this month all were agreed.

"But we must try to foresee all things", continued Ignatius. "It may not be possible to go to the Holy Land. Events are much disturbed. There are constant wars. The seas may not be free, and the routes may be crossed by warring ships. What then?"

Again there was a lively discussion.

In the end, they agreed that if they could not reach the Holy Land within a year after meeting in Venice, they would go directly to Rome and offer themselves to the Pope.

"As a new order?" asked Bobadilla.

"No, as a band of men working together for the glory of God", answered Ignatius. "We are all ready to die, if need be, in God's service."

There was no disagreement among them. The discussion was over, so they followed Favre into the crypt beneath the deserted church. There Favre said Mass. All received Holy Communion. As each one received the Host, he repeated aloud his vows of poverty, chastity, and absolute obedience to the Holy Father. Each made his vow to go to the Holy Land. Each in turn took a vow never to accept money for any work of piety or for giving the sacraments, if and when he was ordained.

It was a solemn moment. Behind them lay many years of preparation. Ahead of them now lay the fulfilment of the mission that had been disclosed to Ignatius in his visions at Manresa. By renewing their vows together, all had again given up the world of passing pleasures for service in the greatest of all causes.

After Mass, they went outside and down the hill a little way. There stood the fountain of Saint Denis. They had brought breakfast with them, and there at the fountain they sat down to eat.

Soon they were chattering and laughing like a group of schoolboys, though they spoke only of their plans to serve God and bring others closer to Jesus in the troubled and evil world in which they lived.

Ignatius sat among them with a little smile of peace

and happiness on his thin lips. He alone knew that the way ahead might be more troubled than the road they had already traveled.

11

THE ROAD BACK TO VENICE

IGNATIUS BEGAN the journey back to Venice long before he had intended to, and by a very round-about way. He left Paris in March 1535 on orders from his doctor, who recommended the cleaner air of Spain. Ignatius had been practicing such penances that he had once more endangered his health. But he would not leave Paris until he had received a certificate from the Inquisitor, Thomas Laurent. This formally cleared him of any doubt about his life, his morals, and his practice of Catholic doctrine.

He went directly to Azpeitia, but he would not go to his brother's castle at Loyola. He went instead to an inn and from there to a spare room at the Hospital of Saint Magdalena. His brother, Don Martin, had learned that Ignatius was coming; someone had recognized him on the way. Wondering why Ignatius had not come on to Loyola, he sent Father Balthazar de Arabeya to talk with him.

Ignatius received the priest kindly, but he would not change his mind about his residence. "Father," he said, "I have taken a vow of poverty. My life must be lived among the poor. Loyola is not a place of the poor. I came back here because I had certain debts to take care of and because I must, if I can, undo the bad example of my youth in this place."

The priest understood his wishes, but Don Martin was hurt. He was even more troubled when Ignatius sent back to Loyola the rich bedding and food that Don Martin had ordered his servants to take to his brother. Ignatius promised, however, to visit the castle before he went away from Azpeitia.

Don Martin came himself to see him.

"What will you do here, Brother?" he asked him.

"I mean to preach to the people for a little while."

"I wouldn't do it. Nobody will come to listen to you here, Brother."

"Nevertheless, I will do so."

Don Martin shrugged. "Ah, well, you were always the stubborn one."

Ignatius had many things to do in Azpeitia. The most important was to set an example of holy living to balance the bad example of his childhood and youth. He preached whenever he could. He preached on the roadsides. He preached in the village square. He even climbed into trees and preached from there. He gathered about him a group of followers to form a Confraternity of the Blessed Sacrament for the relief of those people who were poor but unable to beg, so that they might be given help in secret.

He remained three months in Azpeitia. In that time he called twice to see his brother, Don Martin. Then he turned toward Venice. He still had many duties to perform. He had to go to the family home of Francis Xavier in Navarre, to speak to the Xavier family about Francis' vocation. He had to go to Almanzano, in Castile, to visit the family of Laynez, and to Toledo, to see Salmeron's family. His disciples wanted him to settle some of their business matters. Ignatius himself wished to visit Juan de Castro, who had joined the Carthusian order at Segovia. Only then could he begin to think of going once more to Italy.

In the middle of January 1537, the members of the Company of Jesus met in Venice, as they had vowed to do. At that time, Ignatius had already been there a year. He had spent this year in studying, praying, and giving the Spiritual Exercises. He had added to the number of the disciples one new one—a priest from Andalusia named Diego Hoces.

Their reunion was an occasion of great joy for them all. They sat together on their first day and told of their adventures.

Ignatius, as always, was so modest about his achievements that, if they had not known him better, they would have thought he had done nothing. He told Francis that the Xavier family had been cool to him. "But they are not cold to God, and they are almost reconciled to your vocation, Francis." He had messages for Salmeron and Laynez, too. He spoke of the violent storm through which his ship had passed between Spain and Genoa. He told them of his trip on foot across the Apennines on the road to Bologna.

"It was winter, and I lost the road", he said. "Snow and wind blinded me, and I stood waiting to see where I was. Lo! I was on the edge of a cliff. Whichever way I looked, I could see no path. I could not go back. I could not go forward. There was nothing for me to do but to climb up the face of a steep rock on my hands and knees, with the pit behind me.

"So for once I was facing two pits, for the pit of hell is always before mankind. But it did not please our Lord to let me fall into the pit behind. He allowed me to climb to safety, and then he had his joke at my expense. Just as I came upon a bridge across the stream to Bologna, I slipped and fell off into the water. I was such a sorry sight of mud and water when I clambered up the bank that all those who saw me burst into laughter. After that, I could not collect so much as a penny, even though I begged from one end of Bologna to the other."

Ignatius laughed with his followers at the memory of it.

Favre, too, had had adventures. He had brought along three new companions, whom he had accepted into the Company. Two were ordained—Paschase Broet and Claude LeJay—and one, Jean Codure, was not. There were thus nine of them who had left Paris to come to Venice. They had traveled in time of war. Favre was their leader and was responsible for them. Ignatius had given him this authority when he had left Paris almost two years before. Their dangers were not small, for they had to fear French soldiers, Spanish soldiers, and also the Protestants in the Swiss provinces.

"People thought we were lunatics, to walk in midwinter", said Favre. "Then, before we knew it, we found ourselves in a company of French soldiers. But we were not with them long. A passerby called out, 'Can't you see those men are reformers?' And the soldiers let us go, having no use for reformers, but only for informers.

"Soon, too, we were suspected of being spies. Luckily, we were five Spaniards and four Frenchmen, and we looked like university students, except for our belts and the rosaries we wore. We had our Bibles and breviaries on our backs, and each one had his personal papers. That was all we carried. When we were accused of spying by the French soldiers, why, the Frenchmen among us answered. And when the Spanish soldiers accused us, then the Spaniards in our company answered them. So each time we were freed. And when at last we got to the Protestant villages—why, we always found friends, even though many a time we got into hot arguments with some of their ministers. In one place, a friend led us safely out of a Protestant village on the road to Constance.

"Everywhere God was with us, for here we are—seventeen days earlier than we planned."

The eleven men of the Company now had to decide what to do next. It was winter, so there were no ships sailing for the Holy Land. There would be none until spring. They must find something to do until they could go to Jerusalem.

"Surely there are many charities to be done", said Hoces.

"They are always in need at the hospitals", said Ignatius. "Men are needed to make beds, sweep floors, wash pots. Others are necessary to dig graves and carry coffins, as well as to bury the dead and tend the patients. Couldn't we divide ourselves into two groups? Each group could then serve one of the hospitals in Venice."

All immediately agreed.

"Then, as soon as possible, we must go to Rome for

the blessing of the Holy Father on our journey", said Favre.

Ignatius agreed. "All but me will go", he said.

"Why not you?" asked several of his disciples at once.

Ignatius explained that there were now at the Papal court men who might not be friendly to the mission on which they came if Ignatius were among them. Dr. Ortiz, once of Paris, one of the men who had complained of him to the Inquisition, was now in Rome. Moreover, Cardinal Carafa was now a strong influence in Rome, and he was known to dislike Spaniards; he might act against the Company of Jesus if Ignatius were to go to the Holy City.

"I'll stay here", Ignatius concluded. "After all, it is from here that we sail, and if you can't present our case successfully, then surely I can do no better."

All that winter they labored. They spent long hours in the hospitals. They did without many things. Often they were cold. Even more often they were half-starved. They learned to work without fear of leprosy and the plague. Most of them deliberately exposed themselves to diseases they feared, so that they might learn to conquer fear.

Then, that spring, all but Ignatius set out for Rome. While they were gone, Ignatius continued his charities and prayed. He gave the Spiritual Exercises. And he became more and more anxious as he heard about trouble with the Turks again. He knew that if this continued, they would not be able to make the journey to the Holy Land within the time they had set.

The little band of disciples returned from Rome late that spring. They had good news for Ignatius. Favre told about what had happened to them in the Holy City.

"You would never guess who was our best friend", he said. "It was Dr. Ortiz—none other. It was he who persuaded Pope Paul III to see us. The Holy Father invited us to dinner and told us to talk of divine matters, which we did. He was pleased, and he gladly gave us his blessing. But he said he did not know how we could make the journey, for the Turks have stirred up war again.

"Furthermore, he commanded us to receive Holy Orders. This we are to do as soon as we can present ourselves to a bishop."

"God is good to us", answered Ignatius.

"Even to money", put in Laynez. "See—we've collected over two hundred gold pieces to pay for the trip to Jerusalem."

They knelt together and said a prayer of thanksgiving.

Then Ignatius said, "It is time, my brothers, that we renew our vows. Let us do so before Monsignor Verallo, the Papal Legate. Then the Holy Father will hear from his own legate's lips that we are still determined to serve God."

In obedience to the Pope, those five of them who were not yet priests—except Salmeron, who was too young—presented themselves to the Bishop of Arbe on June 24 of that year. From him they received the sacrament of Holy Orders.

As soon as they were ordained, they separated. It was their intention to go to a place where they were unknown and be alone for forty days. Favre and Laynez went to Vicenza with Ignatius. The others scattered to Monselice, Bassano, Verona, and Treviso.

The two led by Ignatius found a house just outside Vicenza. It was deserted, and it had already begun to fall apart. There were no doors and no windows and nothing but the bare floor for them to rest upon. But they gathered straw for beds. They went out and begged bread to eat. All the rest of their time they spent in prayer and meditation.

At the end of forty days, they met again. The others came to Vicenza. There they worked as before and begged for their food. They performed every charity they could, and, whenever it was possible, they talked to the people of God and gave the Spiritual Exercises. Their goal was still the journey to the Holy Land, which they had vowed to make, if events permitted.

But as the season lengthened into autumn, and then toward another winter, they began to realize that they might not be able to fulfill their vow. The war begun by the Turks still raged. And as long as the Turks controlled the seas to the Holy Land, ships from Italy would not sail. And now the year within which the Company of Jesus has promised to make the journey to the Holy Land would soon be ended.

Once again they gathered together.

"Plainly," said Ignatius, "God has other plans for us. He does not wish us to go to the Holy Land at this time, for the Turkish war continues, and winter is closing the seas. What are we to do?"

Favre reminded Ignatius that they had spoken of going to Rome. "Didn't we decide to go to the Pope and declare ourselves his servants, and then go wherever he wishes to send us?"

"That is true", agreed Ignatius. "But we must learn for ourselves, too, whether our Lord wishes to call any other students to our Company. So, you, Favre, together with Brother Laynez and myself, will go to Rome and surrender ourselves and our Company to the Holy Father. The others among us shall go to the universities of Italy and give the Exercises—Broet and Salmeron to Siena, Lejay and Rodriguez to Ferrara, Codure and Hoces to Padua, Xavier and Bobadilla to Bologna."

To this decision all the Company agreed.

And the last night of his journey, Ignatius had a vision of Jesus carrying his cross.

And Jesus said to him: "I shall be favorable to you in Rome."

12

ROME

WHEN THEY REACHED ROME, Ignatius and his
companions immediately presented themselves
at the Vatican. To their surprise and joy, when word of
their presence was brought to the Holy Father, he
ordered them into his chambers without delay. Pre-
ceded by the Vatican guards, then by the Pope's cham-
berlain, they were shown into the Holy Father's
apartment. When they had bowed before him, they

were even more astonished at the warmth of his welcome.

"I am happy to see you—and especially at last, you, my son Ignatius", he said. "Word of your good deeds has reached me time after time. What can I do for you now? I see you were unable to go to the Holy Land. I did not think events would make it possible."

"Holy Father," said Ignatius, "we have taken a vow to put ourselves at your disposal. As you know, we are a voluntary brotherhood and not an order. We have never thought of ourselves as an order. We vowed together that if it was impossible to make the journey to the Holy Land within a year of our meeting in Venice, then we would come to Rome and be directly subject to your will."

They talked for a little while. The Pope had questions to ask them. When he had heard their answers, he made his decision.

"My son, Ignatius, you, as their author, shall continue to give the Spiritual Exercises", he said. "Brothers Favre and Laynez shall teach, respectively, the Scriptures and scholastic theology, at the College of Sapienza. But are there not others of you?"

"They are to come."

"We shall authorize them to preach in the churches and to instruct in Christian doctrine", said the Pope.

Thus armed with the Pope's approval, they went out into Rome to do as they had been told. The three of them attracted much attention in the city. For one thing, wherever they preached, they spoke Spanish; since their audiences were Italian, neither understood the other. For another, their clothing was new to the people of Rome. For yet another, many people had heard of them even before they arrived in the city. Their reputation grew daily far more rapidly than they liked. Indeed, they would have preferred to remain little known. But this was not to be.

Ignatius especially drew to himself many persons who wanted to make the Spiritual Exercises. Among them were Cardinal Contarini, the ambassador from Siena, and even Dr. Ortiz.

From a visit to Monte Cassino, Ignatius brought back a new disciple, Francis Strada, who had been in the service of Cardinal Carafa. But there were still only eleven in the Company of Jesus, for almost at the same time Ignatius learned with sadness that Hoces had died in Padua.

In the spring of the next year, 1538, Ignatius sent word to all the members of the Company of Jesus to come to Rome. They did so, and soon they were together once more.

They lived in a cottage deep in a vineyard. This had been lent to Ignatius by one of his benefactors. It was so small, however, that they were soon forced to move. This time they went to a more roomy house near the center of Rome. From this house they went forth each day at sunrise to preach and beg.

The notice they attracted was not all favorable.

Ignatius daily expected that attacks upon him and his Company—attacks that are made upon all true followers of Christ—would soon be renewed. He had not long to wait, for that very spring a Lenten preacher accused Ignatius not only of hypocrisy but also of heresy. Finally, someone complained of Ignatius to Governor Benedetto Conversini of Rome, charging him with being a heretic.

Ignatius had endured all kinds of insults and slander ever since the Lenten preacher had first accused him. Now, as month followed month, his patience finally wore thin. Previously he had endured these unjust attacks with meekness; but now he was rightfully angry. He was no longer alone—if he had been, he would have suffered the insults—and it was his obligation to defend those who had become his disciples. With the support of Cardinal Contarini and Cardinal de Cupis, head of the Sacred College, he demanded a hearing.

Those who had accused Ignatius of wrongdoing were quickly shown to be wrong themselves. Indeed, it seemed almost as if God himself had moved in behalf of Ignatius, for some visitors came to the hearing and volunteered to testify for Ignatius and the Company of Jesus. These visitors were no less than the Inquisitors Figueroa of Alcalá, Ori of Paris, and de 'Dotti of Venice, all three of whom happened to be in Rome. Before each of these Inquisitors, Ignatius had been previously tried and found innocent. Faced with such testimony, Governor Conversini found Ignatius and his Company innocent. He ordered, however, that all those who spoke against them should be silent, and that Ignatius and his followers should be silent too.

This verdict was not enough for Ignatius. He was aroused now. He had truly become a soldier of Christ, and he knew that the issue must now be settled once and for all.

He waited until the Pope returned from Nice, and then he went to see him. The Holy Father had already left the Vatican for his villa at Frascati. Not discouraged, Ignatius followed him there. Paul III consented to see him at once.

Ignatius patiently stated his case. He had been examined by the Inquisition in Spain, in France, and in Italy. Each time the verdict was unquestionably in his favor. Yet it had been given in such a manner that it had left room for doubt, and this could not be tolerated.

"Holy Father, is this justice?" he cried. "In Spain and in France and in Italy I was told each time, 'You have done no wrong, but do not do it again.' Now Governor Conversini says we are innocent, but that we should all hold our tongues. We are not to be attacked, but neither can we speak out in our defense. For eight months they have slandered us, and we have stood by. Now surely the people who have listened to these slanders will not know that we are innocent, if they are not told so."

The Pope admitted that this was right.

"No matter how little mud is thrown," continued Ignatius, "some of it will stick. It is time now to wipe this shield clean and begin again."

"You should have appealed the original sentence", said the Pope.

Ignatius smiled grimly, but his dark eyes flashed fire. "Holy Father, I did not have the time; besides, I knew it would be useless. I had no course to take but the one I took."

"It would have been better, in this case, if you had taken the time."

Ignatius again told of the troubles he had had with people who resented the work he was doing and who had brought the Inquisition against him. The Pope listened, questioned, and argued.

But in the end, after an hour had passed, the Pope promised to support Ignatius. He would intervene in the publication of the sentence.

He was true to his word, for when sentence upon Ignatius and his Company was passed, it cleared them of all fault and praised the excellence of their lives and the doctrines they preached. At the same time, it strongly condemned their enemies, especially those who had falsely accused them. And they were permitted to speak out in their defense.

But troubles of another kind soon came.

That winter there was a great famine in Rome. Ignatius and his Company worked night and day for the relief of the poor. They picked up the sick and starving from the streets of Rome and took them to their own house. There they cared for them out of funds contributed by the rich. Sometimes they had more than a hundred people at a time in their house, and they were much too crowded. They gave up their beds, their food, and yet there were always more poor people to be fed. Soon the number of those to whom they gave aid amounted to thousands.

That Christmas, while the famine still raged, Ignatius at last said his first Mass. He had put off this event of great joy because he thought himself still unworthy to celebrate the Mass and because he wanted to prolong the anticipation that the thought of offering the Mass always aroused in him. He went to the Church of Santa Maria Maggiore. He chose for the Mass that chapel which contained the cradle of the infant Jesus. He was so moved by the Mass that tears of joy rolled down his cheeks the entire time.

Soon after, Ignatius and his followers had to face another problem. This arose, in fact, from their very popularity. Because of the great success of the Company, who were known to the people of Rome as the Pilgrim Priests or Jesuits, they were in demand everywhere. One cardinal after another asked for one or two of the Company to be sent to various parts of Europe on special missions. Ignatius soon realized that this would undo the work of his own mission. If the members of the Company were forever to be separated to do the tasks given them by various cardinals, how could they continue to give the Spiritual Exercises and bring people closer to the love of God?

In mid-April of that spring, 1539, all the members of the Company came together again at the request of Ignatius. For several days they fasted and prayed, as always, to prepare themselves to decide the course they should follow.

When they gathered for the meeting, Ignatius pointed out that even now they were being called upon to go to various parts of Italy, France, and Spain. They had placed themselves at the disposal of the Holy Father. So cardinals who wished their help could command it, with the Pope's permission.

"If this continues," went on Ignatius, "while there is no doubt that we are serving God and the Holy Father, at the same time we are not performing our mission. That is because we are not now organized; we are dependent and without a head. We must consider now whether we ought to remain disorganized, or whether we ought to form an organized body."

Every voice was immediately raised in favor of organization.

"But, if we are organized, we must realize that one among us must be the leader of the order. Shall we then add to our vows one of obedience to a member of our Company?"

"We must remember that the people do not favor new orders", said Favre.

"And that the Pope might refuse us permission", added Salmeron.

"And that new disciples may not wish to take such a vow of obedience", said Strada.

"But there are others who will wish to do so", replied Ignatius. "These are matters to be thought about. We shall meet again, and at that time we shall vote on them."

At the next meeting, all their doubts were gone. They were agreed upon the establishment of the new Order. At the same time, they would take a special vow of obedience to the Holy Father. They decided that every member of the Order should instruct in the catechism forty days a year, for about an hour a day. They saw, too, that they ought to choose a superior for life and that any problems should be settled by a majority vote of those members then in Italy.

It was the task of Ignatius to draw up the petition to be presented to the Pope. But what was to be included in it? How should the aims of the Order be set down? The Company sat for hours discussing the things Ignatius should offer to the Holy Father.

First, above all other things, the members of the new Order should be obliged to teach the children of God faith and duty. Second, all new members should make the Spiritual Exercises for three months before becoming novices; afterward they should serve the poor and make pilgrimages. The disciples agreed that, for the time being, the membership of the Company of Jesus should be limited to sixty.

Only after all had agreed upon what was to be set down in the petition was Ignatius free to begin writing it. Even then, the others—now only six with Ignatius because some of the members had been sent by the Pope to Siena and Parma—prepared a summary to guide Ignatius.

"He who wishes to fight for God under the banner of the Cross and serve our Lord alone and his Vicar on earth in our Company, which we wish to be marked by the name of Jesus, should keep in mind that, after a vow of chastity, he is a part of a community that has been founded principally for the advancing of souls in Christian life and doctrine, and of spreading the faith by means of the word, spiritual exercises, works of charity, and specially in the tutoring of children and illiterate persons in Christian principles. . . ."—So it began.

When it was finished, Ignatius called on Cardinal Contarini and asked him to present the document to the Holy Father.

"It will take time," warned the cardinal, "but I do it gladly."

"I will call in a month to learn what has taken place", promised Ignatius.

Four weeks later, Ignatius paid another visit to Cardinal Contarini.

"How was our petition received, Your Eminence?" asked Ignatius.

"The Holy Father read it with great attention", answered the cardinal. "When he had finished, he said, 'The hand of God is in this.'"

"God be thanked!" exclaimed Ignatius fervently.

"But, as you know," continued Cardinal Contarini, "the Holy Father does not act alone in these matters. He sent it to the Master of the Sacred Palace, who is Father Thomas Badia, a Dominican of great learning and saintliness. He studied it very carefully, and he too reported in its favor. The Holy Father then expressed his approval of it.

"But then it came to the Sacred College. There Cardinal Ghinucci, who draws up all the papal papers, raised some questions. To settle them, since I was on the other side, the Holy Father chose as judge Cardinal Guidiccioni. Unhappily, His Eminence is opposed to any new orders. There the matter now stands. We shall need to call those who support you in this cause."

As soon as he returned home, Ignatius ordered special prayers to be said, and he vowed three thousand Masses to be dedicated to a change in Cardinal Guidiccioni's stand. Then he began to write to the friends of the Jesuits.

All this took time, as Cardinal Contarini had said it would.

It was not until September 27, 1540, that the Papal Bull was issued which established the Order of the

Company of Jesus. This was more than a year after the petition had been presented to the Holy Father. In the meantime, Ignatius, Favre, and Laynez had found new recruits for the Company. Pietro Codacio had come from Lombardy; Jerome Domenech from Valencia; Pedro Ribadeneyra from Cardinal Farnese, whom he had served as a page. He had been sent to Ignatius to be punished for misconduct at a dinner given to the cardinals by the Holy Father, and he had remained to join the Company. There were others, but all were soon widely scattered, for the need and demand for the Jesuit Fathers was great on every side.

Once the approval of the Pope was known, the members of the new Order had to elect a superior. Ignatius called all who could come to Rome, and, on March 4, 1541, six of them met. Only Salmeron, Broet, LeJay, Laynez, and Codure came to be with Ignatius. Rodriguez and Francis Xavier had gone to Portugal the year before, but they had left sealed votes to be opened at the election.

For three days the members of the Company of Jesus prayed for guidance.

Then they put their votes in a little box and spent three more days in prayer and meditation.

When the box was opened and the votes counted, it was found that every vote except his own had been given to Ignatius.

Ignatius stood at once and thanked his companions. "But I feel in my soul a greater wish to be governed than to govern", he said. "How can I, who have hardly the strength to rule myself, rule others? I cannot accept this office, and I pray you to consider this matter longer."

They spent four more days in prayer and then voted again.

The result was exactly the same.

This time Ignatius asked permission to seek the advice of his confessor, the friar of San Pietro de Montorio. He made a general confession, adding a description of all his ailments, and asked the friar to order him in God's name either to accept or refuse.

After three days with his confessor, Ignatius was told to accept the vote of his companions.

On the first Friday after Easter of that year, all the Jesuits visited the churches of Rome, and all said their vows in accordance with the provisions of the Bull. In addition, all the others took a vow of obedience to Ignatius, the first superior of the Order of the Company of Jesus.

13

THE LAST YEARS

NOW AT LAST Ignatius felt that he knew God's will. The mission God had revealed to him at Manresa was to be directed from Rome. And he knew, too, that all the traveling he had done before coming to Rome was at an end; his travels were now over. The task that lay before him was so great that it needed all his time and attention. The first problem he faced was that of drawing up a constitution for the Company of

Jesus, but the greatest and most continuing of his obligations was to keep in touch with all the Jesuits, wherever they were.

Soon after his election as superior, Ignatius appointed Jean Codure to be his secretary, knowing he could not do all that would be required of him without help. Codure had expected to go to Ireland, but troubles there kept him at Ignatius' side.

In just a few months, Codure was taken ill. Since he did not improve, Ignatius resolved to say Mass for him at the Church of San Pietro, which was across Rome from the house now occupied by the Order. He set out one morning with two companions—on foot, as always.

But at the Sistine bridge he stopped and said quietly, "There is no need to go on. We are too late. Codure is dead."

They turned and hurried back. Codure had indeed died.

So once again Ignatius was alone with his tasks. In addition to the writings, he insisted on taking his turn at all the most menial chores to be done at the house of the Order. Besides, the writing was very difficult for him. He did not yet know Italian very well, and he made many errors whenever he used that language. Young Pedro Ribadeneyra, in the boldness of youth, scolded him one day.

"Father, you ought to try to improve your grammar", he said. "It's really terrible."

"You're right, Pedro," agreed Ignatius enthusiastically. "Suppose you point out the worst errors to me."

Pedro began at once, with fervor, just as if he himself were not Spanish, like Ignatius. He pointed out the foreign words that Ignatius included among his Italian, and he listed some of Ignatius' mispronunciations. But at length his voice faltered, and he stopped.

"Go on, Pedro", urged Ignatius. "You have only begun."

"I know, Father. But there are so many of them— I'm tired."

"Well, Pedro, what *can* we do for God?" answered Ignatius, smiling.

It was six years before Ignatius appointed another secretary. Then it was a new disciple who seemed intended by God for this very purpose—Juan Polanco, a man who was very nimble with the pen and was capable of long hours of devoted work.

While the Order grew, Ignatius continued to work at the constitution. He had drawn up nine temporary rules, which were to be abided by until a constitution could be adopted. He had done this because, after he had begun the writing of the constitution, he had made many changes. So he could see that it would be many years before he would finish a constitution that could be offered to the Fathers of the Order for approval. Obedience was his first concern, after love of God and the teaching of God and all His works.

After these things, he stressed simplicity of living, next to strength of soul.

His days were filled.

He began each day with a meditation. Then he said Mass, which filled him with such happiness, causing tears to flow so freely, that before long the Holy Father told him to omit his daily Mass, lest he endanger his health. Following Mass, Ignatius spent two hours in prayer, thanking God for His goodness. For a while after that, he either received visitors—for he denied himself to no one—or he went out with one of the Companions to visit the sick or the needy of Rome.

After dinner at noon, Ignatius went into a room set aside for recreation. There he spent an hour with the other Companions. After this, he wrote letters or dictated them to his secretary. Thus he spent the rest of the afternoon. Once supper was over, he listened to reports from those members of the household who had daily tasks to perform. He talked with his secretary about the problems facing the Company of Jesus. At last, at the end of the day, he was alone in his room. There he paced up and down, lost in meditation and prayer, until bedtime, which was always late, for Ignatius had learned to do with only four hours of sleep.

He seldom left Rome.

On one occasion he went to Montefiascone to talk with Pope Paul III about affairs of the Company of Jesus.

Another time he went to settle a quarrel between the people of San Angelo and those of Tivoli. Once more he left the Holy City to go to Naples on a mission for the Holy Father.

The affairs of the Order left Ignatius with little time to attend to matters outside Rome. So he leaned heavily on his Companions. In 1540 he sent Favre to speak for the Catholic cause at the great German assembly, the Council of Worms. In the following year it was Favre again who went to the Council of Ratisbon. From Germany two years later Favre brought Ignatius another new recruit, Peter Canisius. Ignatius sent the Fathers far and wide across Europe, especially to teach at colleges where the Jesuit beliefs might fall upon fertile ground. He sent them to establish colleges of Jesuit learning. When the Council of Trent was called, he directed Laynez and Salmeron to represent the Company of Jesus.

With Laynez and Salmeron, he sent most careful instructions. "Be slow," he told them, "not prompt, to speak in the Council. Be charitable in your opinions and considerate of what others mean to say, even if they have not said it. Take pains to look at the spirit and intentions of the speakers, and in this way learn when to be silent and when to speak. Above all, you must speak in such a manner that you shall not stir dissension but always encourage peace." He studied the reports Laynez sent from the Council with the greatest care, and he laughed when Laynez wrote of how he and Salmeron had been given a little "oven" of a room on their first night in Trent.

Ignatius often felt that he could no longer go on and do justice to the Order he had founded. Once he was driven to write to Laynez and others to tell them of his wish to resign. They met and voted on the matter, but no one could accept Ignatius' resignation; so Ignatius prepared himself to carry on.

He paid as much attention to the most trivial matters of the Order as to its most pressing problems. He found time to establish a house for sinful women and another for converted Jews in Rome. He spent hours with his friend Philip Neri, who was not a member of the Company. Neri differed from Ignatius in almost everything except the love of God. He was light-hearted, and Ignatius was grave; he sang to God, whereas Ignatius prayed to him.

Ignatius continued to write for many years to Francis Borgia, Duke of Gandia, who lived near Valencia, in Spain. The Duke of Gandia had first known Favre and Father Antonio Araoz among the Company of Jesus, and he had written Ignatius to ask that Araoz be permitted to stay in Barcelona. Soon the duke was a close friend to all Jesuits, and when he wished to establish a university for the Jesuits in Gandia, Ignatius gave his permission. Not long after the death of the Duchess of Gandia, Francis Borgia made a vow to enter the Company of Jesus as soon as he could do so.

Ignatius wrote at once to accept the Duke of Gandia. But at the same time, he warned him to be careful, to settle all his worldly affairs, and to be very sure he was not taking a step he would later regret. That so distinguished a leader should renounce the world in favor of the Company of Jesus, instead of one of the older Orders, seemed to Ignatius another mark of God's favor.

In 1546, Ignatius was deeply saddened by the death of Favre. Favre had been chosen by the Holy Father to go to Germany, but illness troubled him. When word of his illness reached Ignatius, he wrote to excuse him from the journey. Favre answered, "A man must obey, but he need not live." Yet he returned to Rome because Ignatius had ordered it. There, in a few days, he died.

Ignatius himself was seldom in good health. Hardly a year went by that did not bring him new sickness. But each year he could see proof of the approval of God, and sometimes he was made especially happy by those who sought him out.

One new follower came to the Jesuit house one day and asked for Ignatius.

"Do you remember me?" he cried, when Ignatius came.

Ignatius did indeed remember him. His eyes lighted. "You are that man who told me one day in a deserted church in Paris that the Bible was enough for you: Jerome Nadal."

"Yes. I rejected you once. I have hardly had a single day without pain since that time. A friend sent me from Rome a copy of a letter written by Master Francis Xavier, and I began to wake up to what our Lord meant me to do. It has led me here. I am ready now."

Ignatius was overjoyed, for he had always had great respect for Nadal and his learning. He kept him close to him, and, after Nadal had been accepted into the Order, he sent him on special missions for which he was well fitted.

But Ignatius' own health did not improve. In 1550, during his Mass on Christmas, he was seized with so serious an illness that he feared he had not long to live. Nevertheless, he made a slow recovery. As a result, he dictated to Polanco a letter to be sent to all the Fathers of the Order. He once again suggested that someone else replace him as superior of the Order.

But, as before, the Fathers refused to elect anyone else to be their superior general.

So, under Ignatius' guidance, the great work of the Company of Jesus went on. By 1551, Ignatius had finished the constitution of the Order. Even so, he was not sure it was ready to be adopted. He insisted that it be examined most carefully and also tested in Spain and other countries.

In this year, too, the Duke of Gandia provided money for the Gregorian University of the Jesuits in Rome. He had already paid for the first publication of

The Spiritual Exercises, the Exercises now at last gathered into the form of a book.

Ignatius attended to all things, but he had always been especially attentive to any of the men who were making the Spiritual Exercises.

A complaint was once made to Ignatius that the procurator of the Order, Ponce Cogordan, was being stingy with the food served to the Jesuits. Ignatius had heard that Cogordan himself had dined on lampreys at the residence of a friendly cardinal. So he called Cogordan to him.

"I hear complaint of you, Ponce", he said. "They tell me you do not even give them decent sardines to eat."

"There's no money, Father", answered Ponce.

"But I have heard you yourself dine on lampreys", Ignatius went on. "Go and buy lampreys for our brethren."

"But the money—!"

"Find the money!"

Somehow he found time to ask the novices to sit with him to talk a little in the garden. He spoke to them often of obedience, but he made sure to add that man gave only rules; God gave the wisdom to abide by them or to disregard them, according to circumstances. The novices, seeking to please him, often brought him roasted chestnuts, which he liked.

Once again, late in 1552, Ignatius was determined to resign as head of the Order. This time he planned to present to the Fathers the man he wished to have follow him. He had long ago decided that Francis Xavier should succeed him. Xavier had set out from Goa for China. Ignatius sent letters after him, recalling him to Rome so that he could offer Xavier in person to the Fathers when he called them together.

But he waited in vain for Xavier. For a long time no word came. And when at last news came from the East, Ignatius could hardly be consoled. Francis Xavier had died of a fever off the coast of China, as he waited on an island for passage to the mainland. Ignatius realized that it was not God's will that he resign; so he resolved never again to try.

Everywhere now the influence of Ignatius and his Company of Jesus was great. Sometimes there were differences of opinion, but there were few problems that could not be solved. The only project that failed was the establishment of Jesuit colleges in the Netherlands.

The Company grew.

By 1555, only fifteen years after the founding of the Order, there were fifteen Jesuit colleges in Spain alone; there were seventeen in Portugal, three in Germany, and two in France. More than a hundred priests had been sent throughout Europe from the college at Rome; more than two hundred others were being trained. In those years, Ignatius had sent out thousands of letters of instruction and guidance to his fellow soldiers of Christ. Yet never once had he failed to attend to the needs of any of the men of the Order closest to him.

In the summer of 1556 Ignatius grew more ill. Even so, whenever the doctors came, he sent them first to other sick Jesuits in the house. He grew steadily weaker because of a lingering fever.

Late in the afternoon of July 30, Ignatius called Polanco to his bedside.

"Go now and obtain the benediction of the Holy Father", he said. "Tell him I am near the end of my life. My work is done."

"Father, the doctors say you have been more ill than this. They see no danger."

"There is nothing for me to do but give up my soul", answered Ignatius. "I know what I am saying."

"Very well. I will go in the morning."

"I had rather you go today, but do what you think best."

That evening one of the doctors and Polanco sat at his bedside to share Ignatius' supper. Another doctor looked in.

"How is he?" asked Polanco.

"I cannot say today. Wait until tomorrow", answered the doctor.

"This is my last evening on earth", said Ignatius calmly.

They talked for a long while about the buying of a new house for the Order in Rome. Ignatius asked many questions, some of which Polanco found hard to answer as fully as Ignatius wanted.

They left him finally to sleep.

Early next morning, during the first hour of sunlight, while Polanco was at the Vatican for the blessing of the Holy Father, Ignatius de Loyola died. He had fulfilled in every detail the mission that God had revealed to him in the visions at Manresa.

AUTHOR'S NOTE

In the interest of historical accuracy, it should be pointed out that Ignatius of Loyola was not baptized "Ignatius". For approximately thirty years of his life he carried his baptismal name of Iñigo (in his admirable book *The Origin of the Jesuits*, Father James Brodrick gives it as Enecus); then, at some time after his conversion, he chose instead to call himself Ignatius, in honor of the holy martyr Saint Ignatius of Antioch. I preferred to avoid using two names for Ignatius in order to prevent possible confusion in the minds of younger readers.

While it is not feasible to set down here a complete bibliography, I should like to say that—apart from the *Spiritual Exercises* of Ignatius of Loyola—I have been greatly assisted in the preparation of this book by *The Origin of the Jesuits*, by James Brodrick, S.J. (Longmans, Green), and *Saint Ignatius*, by Christopher Hollis (Sheed and Ward). I have also been privileged to read Father Brodrick's *Saint Ignatius Loyola: The Pilgrim Years* (San Francisco, Ignatius Press, 1998), surely the most comprehensive treatment of its subject now available to the student.

Finally, I am particularly indebted to Father John La Farge, S.J., who read this book in manuscript and offered excellent suggestions for its improvement.